shadowfalls

shadowfalls

amy kathleen ryan

delacorte press

Published by
Delacorte Press
an imprint of
Random House Children's Books
a division of Random House, Inc.
New York

Text copyright © 2005 by Amy Kathleen Ryan
Jacket illustration copyright © 2005 by Michael Morgenstern

All rights reserved. No part of this book may be reproduced or
transmitted in any form or by any means, electronic or
mechanical, including photocopying, recording, or by any
information storage and retrieval system, without the written
permission of the publisher, except where permitted by law.

The trademark Delacorte Press is registered in the U.S. Patent and
Trademark Office and in other countries.

Visit us on the Web! www.randomhouse.com/teens
Educators and librarians, for a variety of teaching tools, visit us at
www.randomhouse.com/teachers

Library of Congress Cataloging-in-Publication Data

Ryan, Amy Kathleen.
Shadow falls / Amy Kathleen Ryan.
p.   cm.
Summary: After the death of her beloved older brother, fifteen-year-
old Anna is forced to spend the summer with her grandfather in
Wyoming, where she babysits for a traumatized young boy, learns
secrets of her grandfather's past, and encounters a grizzly bear who
seems strangely familiar.
ISBN 0-385-73132-9 (trade) — ISBN 0-385-90164-X (glb)
1. Wyoming—Fiction. [1. Grief—Fiction. 2. Grandfathers—Fiction.
3. Brothers and sisters—Fiction. 4. Family life—Wyoming—Fiction.
5. Mountaineering—Fiction. 6. Bears—Fiction.] I. Title.
PZ7.R9476Sh 2005
[Fic]—dc22
2004009333

The text of this book is set in 11-point Century Gothic CE.

Book design by Kenny Holcomb

Printed in the United States of America

June 2005

10 9 8 7 6 5 4 3 2 1

BVG

Acknowledgments

If my mother had not corrected my grammar so much when I was growing up, I doubt I would be writing these acknowledgments today. My brother, Michael Ryan, has always given me an honest reaction to my writing, pushing me to go farther. My friends Jane Boushehri, Rinnie Orr and Kate Hoffman all helped me early on to believe in Annie's story. Irene Tiersten, my wonderful agent, worked hard to hammer my book into a presentable form, and then found a great home for it. My later readers, Catherine Stine, Tara Morris, and Carolyn MacCullough, were a trustworthy soundboard. Warm thanks to my aunt and uncle, Sharon and Jim Hand, for their title suggestions, which must have numbered in the hundreds. For his relentless perfectionism and pithy e-mails, many sincere thanks to my editor, Joe Cooper. I have deep gratitude for my dearest Richard Weitkunat, who wore his voice down to a nub reading my entire book aloud to me in one weekend. Most of all, though, I must thank my father, Donovan Ryan, for his tireless support and his expert mountaineering advice.

For my family, my origin of stories

Prologue

The sunlight is so bright, shadows seem impossible.

At least, this is how I remember this day.

It's five years ago, but I can still see you up there as clearly as living it. You're clinging to the rock wall, so high you seem only an inch tall. If you fall, your rope will probably catch you. If the piton holding your rope fails, you'll die.

But you don't die today.

Grandpa and I are on the trail below you, holding hands, watching. Gary is at the base of the wall, feeding out rope as you climb. He turns and gives me his sunny smile and a goofy thumbs-up. I return the signal. Gary was such a good guy.

A group of tourists is standing behind us. One man is taking pictures of you with a big camera, a 35-millimeter, the kind I want to use someday. Grandpa turns around to give him a look, but I can tell he's proud.

"To your left," Grandpa calls up to you.

You go right.

Grandpa shakes his head, and I think he's angry until he says, "Beautiful."

I aim my Kodak Instamatic and snap a shot of you hanging off the wall like moss. I can hardly wait until I can climb. There must be pretty good pictures up there.

You stop. You've reached a shelf that juts out from the rock at a forty-five-degree angle, blocking your way. The next handhold over the lip of the rock is way too far for you to reach, and the top of the shelf is too steep for you to stand on. There is nowhere to go.

I'm glad you're coming down soon because we're supposed to go to town for milk shakes at the drugstore.

But you're still hanging under the rock shelf, studying it. Grandpa yells, "That's enough magic for one day!" He seems nervous, and that makes me nervous. Gary looks at Grandpa briefly, then gives your rope a gentle tug, trying to get your attention.

You don't move.

"Can Cody hear you, Grandpa?"

"Probably."

Reaching high above to the lip of the shelf, you pull yourself up with your left arm until your foot can reach your previous handhold. You stay there, stuck, your right arm reaching for a spot that is way beyond you, your left hand at your waist, fingers straining to support your weight. With my free hand, I mimic the position, and it gives me a cramp in my wrist.

The tourists gasp.

You pivot your left hand so that the heel of your palm is supporting your weight. Then you push yourself up until your arm is completely straight and you're leaning over the outermost point of the shelf, bent at the waist. Your feet have left the rock. You're balancing your entire body on one palm while your other hand is casting above for the next hold.

You find it, and pull yourself over the shelf.

I glow with pride. My brother has reached where it was impossible to reach.

"Excellent!" Gary calls up to you. "Wow!"

Grandpa squeezes my hand. I've never seen his eyes look so vibrantly blue as they watch you slither over the rock like a salamander.

One of the tourists behind us, a woman wearing a baseball cap, asks, "How old is that kid?" There is an accusing edge in her voice that I don't understand.

With a sly grin, Grandpa says, "Fifteen."

The woman drops her jaw and walks down the trail, shaking her head.

"Grandpa, am I old enough to start climbing?" I ask him.

"You're pretty small yet, Muffin."

"Cody started when he was ten. I'm almost eleven!"

"Cody's a boy." He thumps one hand on my shoulder, then looks up as you disappear over a swell in the rock. "And Cody's . . . Cody."

I'm silent for a moment as I think about this. "Will I be able to climb like that someday?"

Grandpa glances at me, shakes his head. "I don't think anyone will ever be able to climb like your brother."

I look at Grandpa's face again. He is still studying the spot where you disappeared.

Slowly, I pull my hand away from Grandpa's.

He doesn't notice.

1

The grizzly would find me in the early hours of a high mountain morning.

Grandpa and I began the day on the lazy currents of the Snake River, skirting along the boundaries of the Teton Range in his inflatable raft. The snow-touched peaks looked so tall they seemed to buttress the sky. There was never any religion in my mother's house in Denver, but looking at the Tetons almost made me believe. I wanted to call Cody's name until my voice echoed through the canyons to reach whatever part of him might linger there, but I couldn't. Grandpa wouldn't understand anything so irrational.

Grandpa didn't understand a lot of things. For the entire fifteen years of my life, I doubt he noticed anything about me. Few people did. Mom used to call me her little armadillo, and I didn't mind the nickname until third grade when I finally saw a picture of an armadillo in the encyclopedia at school. It's a gray, squat little animal with a dire expression on its face. I was already painfully shy, but after I realized my own mother saw me as a glorified lizard, I got even worse.

I trailed my fingertips in the water and watched the upside-down world reflected on its surface. The mountains looked as if they were hanging by their roots, dipping into a watery sky. The belly of an eagle flashed across their image, then hung, wings motionless as if caught in a web. Slicing the air with a subtle pivot of its body, it plummeted to annihilate its own reflection. Just as quickly, it burst back into flight with a trout wriggling in its talons. I watched it fly away, higher and higher until it became nothing more than a dark slash across gauzy white clouds.

"Where's your camera?" Grandpa asked, cocking his chin toward where the eagle had flown.

"I left it in Denver," I said quietly.

He was silent for a few moments. Then, pulling heavily on the right oar, he steered us toward a grove of willow bushes along the bank of the river. "Let's cut you a pole."

"What for?"

"Fishing."

"It's not enough that I'm in the boat?"

"You can't lie in bed all day," he said, his chin pointed down.

"Why not?" For the past six months, lying in bed was all I'd done.

"Soon you'll be watching Mabel's grandson. She won't want him inside all day."

"There goes my plan to lock him in a cabinet."

His eyes flicked up to the mountains. He never seemed to get my sense of humor. "Your mother says it'll do you good," he finally said.

No one had even asked me if I wanted the job. When Mabel called us in Denver, Mom had latched on to the idea as if babysitting were the next best thing to Prozac. No matter what I said, her response was always the same: "Your doctor says you need to occupy yourself." She insisted on calling him my doctor even though he was really just the school shrink. I wondered whose feelings she was trying to spare with the euphemism.

When the bottom scraped sand, Grandpa handed me his Swiss Army knife and I waded through frigid water to the willow stand. A deer carcass lay near the bushes, deflated and stiff. Something had been gnawing on it. Its eyes had turned to glass and they stared at me, making me shudder.

I hated any reminder.

I hurried up the bank to find a willow rod that looked straight and strong, and went to work on it. The green wood refused to yield, so I had to saw on it with Grandpa's dull blade, twisting it until the vegetable scent nearly erased the odor of the dead deer. It was hard work, and the sun made me light-headed.

I didn't notice the third odor teasing through the breeze until the wind shifted. It smelled like a mixture of stale urine and rotting meat, a salty tang like beef jerky. It was a powerful stink, but somehow it smelled alive.

I wrinkled my nose and jabbed through the willow switch with the tip of Grandpa's knife. It finally broke away, but the blade caught my knuckle, deep. "Careful," I heard Grandpa say. I ignored him, and sucked on the blood that was pooling in my cut. "Annie."

"It's fine," I snapped, but when I looked at him I realized he wasn't talking about the knife. His eyes were on something behind me. He motioned with one trembling hand, telling me to stay still. I stared at Grandpa, he stared at me, his lips white, brow sweating. I realized he was terrified. A chilly fear washed over me.

Then I heard it. Breathing. A rhythm in the breeze, gusting in and out, deep-chested and deliberate.

Snapping branches and popping twigs, it sounded like a tornado whipping toward me. Fast. Whatever it was, it was *big*. I swallowed air. My body resonated with terror. Though my legs wanted to bolt, I willed them to stay still, repeating under my breath, *Never run never run never run*.

It moved closer still, so close I felt its presence on my skin. I could hear emotion in its breathing—Fear? Rage? Hatred?—faint grunts, little hiccups. It swallowed. I whimpered—didn't mean to, but the sound squeaked out of me.

Oh God, don't let me die here.

Warm breath on my skin.

Puffs of air moved along my forearm, up my back to my neck. I imagined what would come next: quick motion, knocked to the ground, spine bitten clean through. Grandpa would only watch, helpless.

I looked at him again. His icy, pale eyes caught mine. He shook his head because he couldn't say *Never run*.

I flinched.

A cold nose was on my skin, saliva wetting my forearm, meandering along. My knees buckled but I jolted myself stiff. If I went down it might end here.

A tongue flicked at the tender skin of my armpit, curling and gentle, and then again—a slow, languid kiss. It licked me once more, then nudged me toward Grandpa, who stood up, holding a dripping oar like a baseball bat, glaring over my shoulder. "Come on, Annie," he whispered. I didn't move, but he nodded to reassure me, so I took a shaky step, and then another and another, everything in my vision jolting as I struggled through the thick river grass and into the cold of the water. Finally, I fell into the boat.

And Grandpa was pumping the oars, swearing under his breath, rowing frantically until the current caught us midstream. He pointed the bow downriver, and we were away.

Finally I could turn to look.

It was a gargantuan, gnarled grizzly bear. Its winter coat was still shedding, poking from its hide in ropy tufts. It had followed me into the river, its belly dipping in the shallows as it watched after me, paws sliding deep into mud. I met its eyes, tiny brown pinpoints in a huge skull, and it raised its head, flaring its nostrils at the breeze. A memory of a faint dream nipped at the corners of my mind. *I've seen you before.*

We rounded a bend in the river.

I burst into tears.

"You're okay." Grandpa waved his bandanna at me until I took it from him. Tears always made him fidgety.

I wiped my eyes, biting the inside of my cheek until I could stop crying. I concentrated on opening my right hand to release the knife and willow switch that I'd been clutching the whole time. The cut on my knuckle popped open and I closed the bandanna over it, squeezing hard. Grandpa stopped rowing for a minute to look at me. "You're okay," he said again as he closed his big hands around the oars.

"You just sat there." *What would he have done if the bear had attacked?*

"Keep the pressure on that cut." He turned to face the water, glancing at me while I wiped my nose. "Must have been eating on that doe."

"I thought it would kill me."

He turned his eyes onto the Tetons. No response.

I couldn't stop shaking. With one casual swipe of a paw, that grizzly could have broken my neck. I wrapped my fingers around my wrist. It seemed so thin and brittle, so easy to shatter, not that strength really makes a difference. Cody was incredibly strong, and now he was just a pile of frozen flesh lying under the remains of an Andean avalanche.

Six months ago I learned a secret that everybody knows but no one talks about: Death can happen to anyone, for any reason, at any time. It had happened to Cody, and now it almost happened to me. For a few minutes, a dumb grizzly bear had the power to decide whether I lived or died.

"There's extra line in the tackle box," Grandpa said, waving astern.

Apparently my near annihilation wasn't enough to derail Grandpa's brilliant fishing plan.

I couldn't work my fingers around the line, so Grandpa took it from me and knotted it around the top of the willow switch, pulling the end tight with his teeth. He fixed a shiny yellow lure to the other end, and pushed the ridiculous contraption at me until I finally took it from him.

I held my stupid homemade pole, wishing I was home in Denver, in my bed with nowhere to go, nothing to do. I stared into the river at my reflection. My eyes looked huge, my hair haphazard and tangled, my skin the color of gray water.

Upside-down Annie in an upside-down boat with a backwards Grandpa, trailing a hook, hoping to kill an unsuspecting fish.

2

I hooked three trout. Grandpa released the first two, skinny fish that would be better eating in another season, but he kept the third, a handsome twelve-incher. As he gutted it over the side he said, "We'll give this one to Ned for the ride back." After watching Grandpa yank out its guts, I was glad I wouldn't have to eat it.

By the time the Wilson Bridge was in sight, it was well past lunchtime. Grandpa steered the boat toward the steep dike, and we both got out to tug the raft onto land. I left him to deflate the sides and jogged up the road to the last restaurant before Teton Pass led into Idaho farmlands. Nora's Fish Creek Inn was town hall, bus station and watering hole for the hamlet of Wilson, Wyoming. I could smell the green chilies from across the highway. Nora serves the best huevos rancheros in the valley.

Inside it was so dark after the bright summer light I had to wait for my aching eyes to adjust. I sat down at the U-shaped counter in the center of the room and turned my mug right-side up. The place was full and noisy as the lunch crowd sipped their midday coffee. Some people recognized me and nodded, and I could see a few whispering as they looked at me. No doubt the news about Cody had made its circuit in the six months since the phone call. It followed me everywhere, from the newspapers in Denver to where the Snake River nudged the shoulders of the Tetons. If one more person came up to me to say what a hero my brother had been, I thought I might lose my mind. To me, heroes were the ones who made it out alive. Anyone who didn't was just a victim.

At least in Jackson I was safe from that kind of sympathy. Folks who lived in this valley preferred keeping to themselves. Though I'd seen these people every summer of my life, we never really progressed beyond the nod hello. Like Grandpa, most residents of Jackson Hole looked for their community in the wilderness, away from people. Though he'd lived here all his life, I could count Grandpa's real friends on one hand. Not that he talked to them much.

Nora, the owner of the inn, was one of our friends. She rushed up and filled my coffee cup. "Annie! You been here a whole two weeks and your grandfather is just bringing you by?" I smiled. I always liked Nora's gravelly country voice. "Wants you all to himself, that Jack McGraw! I ought to give him what for!"

"Hi, Nora." I was grateful that she didn't mention Cody.

She rubbed my back a little, then hurried off to the other tables to hide the fact that she was near tears. I knew it was hard for her to see me without him. Cody was one of her favorite customers. She always used to tease him about how handsome he was, and he always replied with, "You're all talk, Nora, but will you ever deliver the goods?" Then they would mock-flirt almost to the point of obscenity. It always embarrassed Grandpa because everyone in the restaurant would laugh at them.

A lot of people missed Cody.

A strange noise behind me made me turn around. A boy a little older than me with brown hair and dark eyes was spinning a coffee cup on his table. The sound echoed rudely through the restaurant, and people nearby turned to look. He met the glare of an old woman and pointedly spun the mug again, even harder. Coffee sloshed over the rim and onto his T-shirt, but he didn't seem to care. There was something in his posture that seemed to embrace the suckiness of life, and to me that made him seem more honest than most people. His eyes found mine, and he stopped spinning the mug. I realized I'd been staring, so I raised my menu to hide my face. When I peeked over the top again, he was still looking at me, but this time he was smirking.

I turned back to the counter, pretending to be utterly engrossed in the fascinating menu.

Grandpa came in with a bang of the screen door. He surprised me by nodding to the cute mug spinner, who nodded back and said, "Hello, Mr. McGraw."

"Marcus," Grandpa said as he sat down. To my horror, he pointed at a stool between us. "Have a seat."

"No thanks, I'm on my way out." He stood, tall and lean in faded jeans and a torn T-shirt. The corners of his mouth pricked upward. "You're Annie?"

"Uh-huh" was all I could manage. How did he know my name?

"Are you coming to the picnic on Sunday?" Grandpa asked him.

"Yeah."

"Your mother too?"

"Yeah," he muttered, casting his eyes downward. "She'll be in town for a few days."

"Good to hear," Grandpa said with an encouraging nod.

I was even more mystified. The boy looked at me

from under heavy bangs that nearly covered his eyes. "Nice to meet you."

"Th-thanks," I sputtered. This was my curse: The cuter the guy, the dumber I sounded.

He nodded again as he dropped some bills on the table. With three long-legged strides, he was out the door.

"Who was that?" I tried not to let my voice show any interest.

"Zachary's older brother," Grandpa said as he took the stool next to me.

"Zachary?"

"Mabel's grandson."

"Oh yeah." Sunday we were going to the Wilson Firemen's Picnic so I could meet the kid I was being forced to babysit for the summer.

"Zachary is shy," Grandpa said, "so—"

"I should wear my clown suit?"

"Mabel's been a help to me."

"Uh-huh."

"Your mother wants you to keep busy."

"Why can't Mabel watch him?"

"She's managing the candy counter at the drug-store."

"Just what she needs, access to free candy."

"Don't be cruel."

Nora came over to take our orders. Grandpa asked for the usual and I ordered my huevos, and then Grandpa got up to find Ned the cook, our ride home. Through the swinging kitchen door I caught snips of their conversation: "big old bear . . . took a taste . . . never so scared . . ." Ned stood holding his huge metal spatula, his lantern jaw hanging to make his face look even longer. At the end of the story Grandpa came back out with a sly grin. "Your bear has old Ned speechless."

"How do you know it was a male?" I asked.

"Powerful animal."

"Girl grizzlies are puny?"

"You were cool-headed today," he said as he raised his mug to his lips. Before taking a sip he added, "There's McGraw blood in there somewhere."

I bowed my head so he wouldn't see how hurt I was. Maybe he was trying to tell me he was proud of me, but the way he said it felt like a door closing in my face. The McGraws have always been tall, proud, athletic people with eyes the color of blue crystal. I'm small, totally insecure, and my eyes are such a dark brown that you can't tell my pupil from my iris. I'd always thought of myself as an outsider. Apparently, Grandpa saw me that way too.

I stared into my coffee mug, but a feeling of being watched made me look up. An old man, probably a Shoshone or Arapahoe from the Wind River Reservation in central Wyoming, was looking at me. He sat across from us at the opposite arm of the counter. His face was carved like a tree stump, his skin leathered and brown from the sun. He nodded as if he recognized me. His stare was so intense that Grandpa noticed. "Haven't seen a grizzly that big in years," Grandpa said, and set down his coffee as his gaze wandered again to the old man, who was still squinting at me. I was starting to feel creeped out.

Grandpa has a way of making a normally polite question sound like a threat. "Something I can do for you, friend?"

The man's eyes twinkled as he grinned good-naturedly. "You can tell me the story of the grizzly and your granddaughter."

"Eavesdropping a habit of yours?"

The man laughed. "Only when the story is good."

Grandpa looked him over, then shrugged. "Annie can tell it."

"Grandpa!" I whispered to try to stop him, but it was too late. The man was already picking up his coffee mug and ambling around the counter. He took the empty stool next to me and sat, hands folded, staring straight ahead. He was old, but his motions were deft and concentrated.

I waited for him to ask something, but he only nodded.

"Well, I was, uh," I sputtered, "s-standing on the riverbank, and a bear snuck up behind me."

He took a sip of coffee, eyes still fixed ahead. "What did the bear do?"

"He sort of sniffed me."

"Then what?"

"He licked me."

He raised his eyebrows, but still didn't look at me. "Licked, how?"

"I don't know." I rubbed my arm where the bear's tongue had grazed me. "Like when a dog kisses you, you know?"

"Uh-huh."

"And then he grunted a little, and pushed me."

"Knocked you down?"

I could still feel it, a shove on the small of my back, just enough force to set me in motion. "No, just sort of nudged me a little."

"Then what?"

"I got in Grandpa's raft and we left."

"What did the bear do?"

"He followed me into the river and watched us leave."

"Watched you how?"

"He just . . . stared at me." *Like you were staring,* I wanted to add, but that would have been rude.

"He stared at your face?"

"Right at my eyes." *His brown eyes on mine, watching after me as I floated away.*

He nodded, took a slow sip from his coffee, set the mug down and folded his hands again. "How did that feel?"

I looked at Grandpa, who rolled his eyes. "I don't know," I said. "I was scared, but . . ."

"Yes?"

The man looked in my eyes. Again I heard the whispers that had woven through the dappled light between the bear and me. *I've seen you before. I know you from the forest of the black, black trees.* "It felt . . . familiar," I mumbled.

He nodded, and sat there in silence, thinking. I stared into the dark of my coffee until the old man cleared his throat. "Great-Grandfather is watching you."

I gaped.

Grandpa leaned in. "Pardon?"

"Your granddaughter has a powerful friend."

The man grinned. I had a vague sense he was playing a part, teasing us somehow.

"Well, her friend almost ate her," Grandpa said.

The man paid no attention to Grandpa. "The grizzly was here long before people came to this continent. That's why he's called Great-Grandfather. In some legends his spirit is the strongest of all animal spirits. If Great-Grandfather is your ally, he'll watch over you." I must have been looking at him like he was a lunatic because he laughed and slapped my shoulder again. "It's a good sign." He plopped some change onto the counter and walked out the door.

Nora rushed by with two plates of food and whispered to Grandpa, "It's on the house, Jack, compliments Ned." Grandpa winked at her and took a huge bite of his sandwich. He said to me through a mouthful of corned beef, "Looks like you have yourself a totem."

"A what?"

"Animal spirit."

I couldn't tell if he was serious or not. I picked up my

fork and poked at my food, too stirred up to eat. I kept seeing that scruffy bear on the bank, glowing in the sunlight, watching me go. *Why did you let me go? Why didn't you kill me?*

Grandpa ate quickly, then left me to pick at my huevos while he took Ned's truck to load up the raft. He was gone a long time, so I finally pushed the cold plate away and went to sit on Nora's porch to wait. The air was cooling down, and I could hear the distant clang of pots and pans as Ned cleaned up for the evening.

Birdsong fluttered through the breeze, and I listened to hints in the chatter. When I was a little girl, spending long days alone with my camera waiting for Grandpa and Cody to come back from climbing, I discovered that you can tell when a bird is angry, or scared, by the way it sings. Sometimes they'll even signal the approach of an animal. Because of the frantic peal of a jay, I once got a great picture of a fox as he scurried past me. When I was younger, I used to put words to birdsong, stupid dreamy lyrics about fairies and princes and lost kingdoms. That evening on Nora's porch, I imagined the birds trilling about the bear who kissed a girl but lost her to the river.

The screen door banged and all the birds flew away.

It was Ned, done with his day's work. He pulled out a Marlboro Red as he sat on the steps next to me. "Saw you talking to that old Indian," he said.

"Yeah."

From his breast pocket, he pulled a lighter with a picture of the American flag on it. "Did he say what reservation he comes from?"

"No."

"Probably Wind River."

"I guess."

"Don't often see 'em up here."

"He seemed okay."

"He's been coming around here a lot," he said as

he sparked a flame and held it to his cigarette. "I ever tell you the time I got jumped by a bunch of 'em down in Riverton?" He blew out a stream of smelly smoke. "I bagged a nice little antelope and they didn't like that. Accused me of hunting on the reservation. They don't put up no signs, so how you supposed to tell? I told 'em I got it on BLM land. That didn't stop 'em from kicking the sh—" He stopped himself. "Pardon. Kicked the crap out of me. Left me in the parking lot. Cold that night. Lucky someone came along."

"Yeah."

"They have a different attitude when they're on their own. More polite."

"I guess."

"It's that whiskey. Makes 'em mean."

"Whiskey makes everyone mean," I said.

Ned merely nodded uncomfortably.

I didn't bother telling him that my father had been a quarter Blackfoot. It would have embarrassed him. Besides, Ned probably would have used my wayward father as evidence that our "kinds" shouldn't mix. Dad left us when I was barely three, so long ago that his memory was only the smoke I'd smelled on him. As for my being Blackfoot, the only way you could tell is the color of my eyes and hair. Otherwise I look completely white. Besides, I'd never even been to a rendezvous, so it seemed pretentious to claim native roots.

Grandpa finally tooled up and I squeezed into the backseat of Ned's truck. I dozed all the way to the cabin while the two of them talked about bears and fishing and that time Ned got jumped outside a bar in Riverton.

3

After we unloaded the raft and Ned drove off, Grandpa stocked the small woodstove in the corner of the living room. In this secluded valley, even in the middle of June, the nights are cold enough to freeze dew on the weeds. Grandpa burned wood trimmings he picked up while clearing the trails around the cabin. The circle of groomed paths around his place got smaller every year as his joints got stiffer. The forest was slowly taking over. There was a time when the trails were the only way to get from one settlement to another, and all the inhabitants of our nook in the valley helped out. Now it seemed Grandpa was the only member of the aging population who cared about the trails anymore. Everyone else drove to visit neighbors.

The cabin walls were made of settled logs the color of pitch, but most of them were hung with quilts my grandmother had made. When she died twelve years ago, she left behind squares of color flowing over every surface of the room. Blue and violet calico covered the sagging couch under the front window. The armchair Grandpa usually sat in was draped in different shades of denim cut from old jeans. The rocking chair that marked the border between the living room and the kitchen was decked in alternating lilacs and rosebuds. Even the curtains were made of quilts and trimmed with lace.

I was about to go up the ladder to the loft, but Grandpa stopped me. "Annie, sit down for a second."

He settled himself into the squeaky armchair. I sat down on the end of the couch and fidgeted. Grandpa never initiated conversations. In the two weeks I'd been in Jackson, our talks had been limited to intelligent observations about the weather.

"You should know something about Zachary."

"Okay."

"He's had a pretty tough time this year. Mother is in a mental hospital in Pocatello. That's why the boys are here."

This got my attention. "What for?"

"Swallowed some pills." He paused, letting this sink in, then said, "She's fine. In treatment for alcohol. Depression. Resident program."

"Seriously?"

"They're letting her out this weekend to visit the boys, so it can't be too bad." He looked at me intently. "It's just . . . Zachary might need some special care."

"Great." Now I was really angry at Mom for roping me into this. I felt sorry for the kid, but I had my own problems to deal with. Besides, I'd never been good with children. I'm not one of those peppy people who make babies giggle. I hate the way they stare at you; they seem to cry too easily and I never know how to calm them down. If this was how I felt about normal kids, how could I help a kid with real problems? "Grandpa, I don't know if I'm the right person for this."

"Mabel thinks you'll do fine."

"I know, but . . ."

"Your mother made the decision. I have to back her up."

"Why don't I get any say in this?"

"That's a question for your mother. You should call anyway, before it gets much later," Grandpa said as he went to the bathroom.

Apparently, our conversation was over.

I sat there, listening to Grandpa brush his teeth, wishing for a way out, not just from babysitting, but from this place. Traces of memory clung to every surface in the room. Cody sitting on the couch reading *Endurance* for the hundredth time. Cody opening the refrigerator every two minutes for yet another dill pickle. Cody practicing knots with Grandpa at the rough pine table in the kitchen, talking about this expedition or that mountain while I quietly read my book. Being here just made Cody seem more gone.

"Call your mother," Grandpa said again as he turned off the bathroom light and went to his bedroom.

"I am!" I struggled up from the couch. Holding the antenna of the cordless phone in my teeth, I stomped up the ladder to the loft, slumped on my creaky cot and dialed home.

"Mom, it's me."

"Hi, sweetheart." Her voice was taut. I could tell she was forcing herself to sound cheerful, probably for my sake. "How's my girl?"

"Fine," I said, purposefully keeping my voice in its usual depressed tone. Her false moods were harder to take than her devastation.

"Did you go on the river today?" she asked, still chipper as a beauty contestant.

"We saw a bear."

"Black?"

"Grizzly."

"I bet you wish you'd had your camera. I saw you forgot it in your room."

"I'm not into it anymore."

"That's crazy! You've been into it since you were old enough to read the instructions."

"Not anymore."

"I'll send it to you."

"I don't need it."

"But you're in Wyoming. You're missing all the animals."

I looked at the picture hanging over the dresser next to my cot. It was an eight-by-ten of a moose mother and her calf grazing in a marsh. I remembered taking that photo. Mama was dipping her head into the water looking for soggy greens, and her baby was watching her intently, learning. Mama would pull up mouthfuls of plants, buckets of water sloughing off her as she chewed. Her calf finally tried dipping its own head into the water, but came up sneezing. I had to work hard to hold in my laughter when I snapped that frame. For me, photography wasn't just about taking pictures of animals. I tried to show how much like humans animals can be. They teach their babies. They worry. They love.

Now photography just didn't seem important anymore. After what happened to Cody, nothing did. "I've taken enough pictures," I said. Mom said nothing, so I changed the subject. "What are you doing?"

"Just sitting here in the dark. . . ." All her cheeriness was gone. She sounded so pathetic I wanted to hang up, even though this was nothing new. I would come down from my room at all hours of the night and find her sitting at the kitchen table, staring into the darkness, her blue eyes drained and bloodshot, her curly gray hair sticking up in wild, wiry bunches. Mom hadn't gotten much sleep since the phone call. Sleep was all I'd done since. "Are you and Grandpa having a good time?"

"Yeah," I muttered in a way that really said no.

"Make yourself available to him, Annie. You might be surprised."

"I'm trapped with him in a cabin in the middle of nowhere. I'm available."

"You know what I mean."

"He's just so . . ."

"I know he's gruff, but that's just on the outside, Annie. He loves you very much."

"And I don't see why I have to babysit that kid. Did you know his mom's a wacko?"

"I went to high school with Penny; she's not a wacko."

"She tried to kill herself."

"That might have been an accident."

"I don't want to do this."

"It's not up for discussion."

"I don't have the energy, Mom."

"You're doing it, and that's final, Annie." Even through her weariness, her voice had that immovable McGraw timbre.

"I don't see why I have to." I tried to sound just as firm, but my voice came out whiny.

"You've got to learn to be in the world again, Annie."

"What does that even mean?"

"Your brother—" She tripped up, unable to complete the thought. Mom hadn't uttered his name in months, at least not to me. Anytime he came up, one of us changed the subject. "You have to learn to forge your own way."

"Uh-huh."

"You can't give up on Grandpa just because . . ."

". . . Cody was his favorite?"

"That's not true!" She seemed furious, maybe because of what I'd said about Grandpa, or maybe because I'd dared to speak Cody's name. "They were just . . . climbing buddies."

"Yeah, right." Climbing buddies—as if it had been a casual hobby. Other kids played basketball or football or baseball, but Cody had to be the rock climber. Even after our good friend Gary died, victim to a thirty-foot fall from a rock wall, Cody still had to risk his life every damn weekend, and no one in my family ever gave it a second thought. Except for me. "I don't want to climb," I said sharply. "It's too dangerous. I don't know why you ever wanted me to."

"What are you talking about?" She was steaming now, but it was a relief from her zombie routine. "You used to beg to learn!"

"And *still* no one let me. I don't see why it was too dangerous for me and not for—" I couldn't finish the thought.

"What are you saying?"

"I'm saying I'm not going to climb."

"No one said you have to climb. Just talk to your grandfather. You need him."

I lay with my face in my pillow, too angry to say anything but "I have to go."

"He loves you, Annie."

"Good night." I hung up before she had a chance to reply. I held the receiver in my hand, sure she would call back and scold me for being rude, but the phone never rang.

I felt farther away from Denver than ever, and the night outside seemed even darker.

I went back downstairs to brush my teeth and change the bandage on my throbbing finger. While I was in the bathroom I thought I heard the ladder to the loft creaking, but when I came out Grandpa was in his bedroom, buttoning his pajama top. It was the red plaid set Cody had given him for Christmas two years ago.

There wasn't anything about being here that didn't remind me of Cody.

Grandpa winked at me—something he hadn't done in years—and said in the booming tone he used when trying to pass as cheerful, "Round of Chinese checkers?"

My throat locked as I remembered laughing with Cody, chasing stray marbles. "It's no fun with just two," I answered.

Grandpa's eyes faded and he seemed to forget the top three buttons on his nightshirt. "Okay," he murmured. "Good night, Annie."

"Night." I turned away from his disappointment and climbed back up the ladder.

I sat on my cot, looking at the room. Everything was just as we'd left it last year. It hurt to see all our things the same, as if Cody were still here. The day I arrived for the summer, I thought about putting away all signs of him, but it would hurt worse to disturb them. Besides, it was useless. There was nothing I could do to make the ache go away.

One of Cody's old climbing harnesses hung from a hook in the corner. His scratched compass sat on the windowsill, collecting dust. And his pictures. His dozens of pictures coated the wall and the ceiling over his half of the room.

I used to hate Cody's pictures—all clippings from outdoor magazines—of mountaineers buckling under huge packs in thin air, or ice climbers scaling glaciers with their crampons and ice axes. Just looking at those photos would give me vertigo, but Cody used to lie on his cot and stare at them every night. Sometimes he would talk to me about what the climbers were doing, why they chose this particular knot or that particular piton or other kinds of rope anchors. I'd ignore him, trying to read my books, but sometimes he would draw me in and I would have to stop reading and listen to him talk about where he wanted to climb, who he wanted to climb with.

Last summer, I thought he would never shut up about the Argentina expedition. He yammered on endlessly about how they would trek miles into the forest, and then miles above it, so high in the mountains not even moss could grow. That is where my brother wanted to live, in air so thin it couldn't even keep plants alive.

In the center of the pictures was Cody's greatest prize. *Outside Magazine* had done a feature story about him and Grandpa, and their picture was on the cover, their weathered features grinning at the camera. There was a black-and-white inset of my great-grandfather holding a huge coil of hemp rope. Below the pictures, in large, red letters, was a caption that read, "Three generations of McGraw mountaineers." I'd watched from the sidelines as Cody and Grandpa posed for the photographer.

The day that issue came, Cody pored over every word of the article, and then he read it aloud to Grandpa and me as we sat at the kitchen table drinking lemonade. Cody carved the cover off with an X-Acto knife and took down a framed picture of him and me from a couple summers before. He slipped the magazine cover over our picture. It didn't bother me at the time, but now when I thought about it, I wondered why he had to cover up our image like that. So easily. As if that moment in time when we were both well and happy didn't matter at all.

That magazine article got him into the Argentina expedition. The team leader figured his presence would bring in endorsements to fund the trip, and it did. I hated looking at that picture.

I took the frame off the wall, ignoring Cody's voice in my head that whispered, *Don't touch that, it's not yours.* I pulled the back of the frame off, yanked out the magazine cover and ripped it into a hundred pieces. I was ripping up a part of Cody, but I didn't want to keep this piece of him. It was the piece that couldn't get enough attention or adventure, the piece that had gotten him killed. I replaced the back on the frame, hung it up again and studied the picture that had been hidden. Cody and I looked back at me, a moment from three summers before. His light brown hair, bleached blond by the sun, hung in his pale eyes. He had draped one muscled, tawny arm around my shoulders, and I was smiling at the camera, my hair in a ponytail, my brown eyes sleepy-looking. That was the Annie before she knew Cody was temporary. I stared at her as though she were a stranger.

I got into bed and rolled onto my side to face the other wall. My hand grazed something cool and hard under my pillow and I pulled it out. It was a bear pendant carved from red jasper, hanging from a leather thong. Grandpa must have bought it at the little Indian jewelry store across the highway while Ned and I talked on Nora's porch.

I thought about what Grandpa had said at the inn. *There's McGraw blood in there somewhere.*

I slipped the bear pendant into the drawer on my nightstand.

I turned off the light and buried my face in my pillow. Two more months alone with Grandpa, trapped in this aching cabin. While I was in Denver with Mom I could pretend Cody was here in the mountains, sleeping in the loft, going on day trips with Grandpa. But now that I was here, the truth was plain. Cody wasn't anywhere. He was just gone.

4

Grandpa's still looking for you.

Two weeks ago, when I first stepped into the airport, Grandpa looked past me, over my shoulder, waiting for you to appear. He seemed to catch himself, gave me an embarrassed smile and a quick hug. We went to find my luggage.

We hadn't seen each other since your funeral because he'd left straight from the cemetery. He didn't even say goodbye to Mom and me, really. As soon as the minister uttered "Amen," he turned on his heel like a mechanical toy soldier, marched to his pickup and drove off. We were still waiting for him in our living room at eleven o'clock that night. Mom sat, withered, under a tattered yellow quilt Grandma had made for her when she was a baby. I was sitting straight-backed in our big easy chair, still in my coat, staring at the door, expecting Grandpa to walk through it with some explanation. It was Mom who finally figured out he was already driving home to Wyoming. She forgave him so easily for that.

My first night here, Grandpa took me for dinner at

the Sweetwater Grill, your favorite restaurant. If you'd been with us, you would have told Grandpa all about the climbs you'd done in the Colorado Rockies over the fall, winter and spring. When dessert came, you would have smeared a huge glob of chocolate mousse over your lips and then asked, deadpan, "Annie, do I have anything in my teeth?"

With you along, dinner would have taken two hours, but Grandpa and I were finished in less than forty-five minutes. We ate quickly, quietly. He asked me a few questions about Denver and Mom, but I don't think either of us heard my replies. We didn't order dessert.

During the long drive to the cabin, I thought about how there must be degrees of silence just like there are degrees of temperature. When I used to give you the silent treatment for teasing me too much, that was like the freezing point of water. Driving to the cabin through the summer evening, the silence between Grandpa and me was absolute zero, as if we were on Pluto, so far from the sun that its warmth couldn't reach us. I guess that makes you the sun.

When we got to the cabin Grandpa looked at the wall clock and said it was getting late, even though it was only nine-thirty. His eyes looked red. In a jagged voice he told me good night, and closed the bedroom door behind him.

I climbed the loft ladder without turning on any lights. Head down so I wouldn't have to look at your things, I undressed and crawled under the covers. I curled my pillow around my ears so I wouldn't hear the crickets, trying instead to imagine the traffic noise that would come through my bedroom window in Denver.

All through the plane ride, and picking up my luggage, and dinner, and the drive, I could hardly wait for this moment, to get into bed and hide away from the *world. Since the phone call, bed has been my only escape. But when my head hit the soft, cool pillow, I didn't feel relieved at all. What worked in Denver doesn't work here. You should be in the cot across the loft, keeping me awake, making me laugh until your words dissolve into snores. If you were where you belonged, Grandpa could stop looking—and I could stop listening—for you.*

I'm still talking to you, though, whispering into the dark, sending prayers to you like weak beams of light to be swallowed by a big nothing at the other end.

If there were a temperature colder than absolute zero, this would be it.

5

Somehow firemen seem eminently qualified to host a barbecue. At the annual Wilson Fire Department Benefit Picnic people can come and eat all the bird they can stuff into themselves while listening to the best amateur bluegrass music in Wyoming. (Which isn't saying much.) Cody and I always used to look forward to the picnic. He came to flirt with the girls; I came for the chicken. This year I dreaded the picnic because it would be another first without Cody, and I dreaded every first. The first Christmas without Cody. My first birthday. My first trip out to Grandpa's. The first firemen's picnic.

As soon as we got there, Grandpa was outflanked by a group of starstruck young climbers. They wanted him to tell them about some winter ascent or other, which suited me just fine. I needed some time alone.

I was sitting in the shade of a cottonwood tree away from the crowd, chewing my way through a wing, when I spied Marcus with a little boy, a short, pale version of himself. That must be Zachary. They were standing in the lemonade line. Marcus was even better looking than I remembered, in a black T-shirt that deepened his dark eyes, and baggy jeans. I ducked my head over my plate, hoping he wouldn't see me.

I'm shy when I first meet anyone, but cute guys turn me into a total mute. When I was twelve, Cody and I ran into one of his hot climbing buddies, a tall guy named Rich with gorgeous big teeth and soft brown hair. After talking to Cody for about twenty minutes, he finally noticed me standing there and asked me how I was doing. I stared at him trying to think of a response until he asked Cody with real concern, "Dude, is your sister deaf?" So I was really nervous about having to talk to Marcus, and I hoped Mabel would show up soon. She could dominate any conversation.

Still, I was curious, and watched as Marcus slowly moved through the lemonade line. He seemed totally unaware that his little brother had his finger looped through his rear belt loop. I liked how Marcus seemed to take it for granted that he was his brother's protector. That was how Cody had been with me when I was little.

Marcus spotted me and waved an uncertain hello. He muttered something to Zachary, who looked at me with trepidation. Loaded down with two full paper plates, two cups of lemonade and his little brother, Marcus slowly started toward me. I had plenty of time to get really anxious, and assumed my usual armadillo posture: curl spine for protection from incoming blows, speak very little, move with extreme stealth.

He smiled crookedly and said, "Good to see you again."

"Hi." I folded my arms over my chest, unfolded them, and folded them again. Desperately I scanned the crowd. Grandpa was still trapped in a mesh of eager young climbers. Mabel was nowhere.

I was going to have to handle this alone.

"Zachary, this is Annie," Marcus said as he carefully

set the plates on the log next to me. "Annie's taking care of you tomorrow. Isn't that cool?"

The little boy lifted his opaque eyes to me. I tried to smile at him, but there was no response or recognition in his look, just a long, steady stare. It was spooky.

"Pleased to meet you," I mumbled as I unfolded my arms again.

Marcus tried to get Zachary to sit on the log next to me, but the little boy shook his head vehemently and backed away. Finally Marcus got him to sit cross-legged on the ground not less than ten feet away, his plate balanced on his lap. Zachary glanced at me once, and then away quickly as if my face were hurting his eyes.

This kid was seriously messed up. What had Mabel gotten me into?

Finally, Marcus sat next to me, his plate between us on the log. He took a big bite out of his hamburger. "You enjoying the picnic?" he asked just as the band broke into a rendition of "Dueling Banjos."

"Yeah," I said, more flatly than I'd intended.

To him it must have sounded sarcastic, because he chuckled before biting into a big stack of potato chips.

I tried to think of something to add, but came up with nothing. Nada, zilch, zero. I had no idea how to keep a conversation going with him. "Where's Mabel?" I asked, trying to sound casual.

He cocked his head toward the parking lot. I saw her sitting in the passenger's seat of a little green car I didn't recognize, her puffy red face sweating under the curls of her blued hair. In the driver's seat a pale, thin woman—who I realized must be Penny—was angrily tapping her cigarette out the window, shaking her head.

"Is that your mom with her?"

He nodded grimly.

"Why don't they come out for some food?"

"They're having a fight." Marcus's voice was as sharp as the fiddle in the bluegrass band.

"Is everything okay?" I asked.

Marcus shook his head and took another huge bite of his hamburger.

I looked over to see that Grandpa had struggled through the crowd of young climbers that had surrounded him and was trying to join the lemonade line. He shot a desperate glance at me as an older guy in a big Stetson hat came over to him and patted his shoulder.

"Your granddad seems popular," Marcus observed.

"Yeah," I said, and then stalled, trying to come up with something witty. I looked at Zachary, who was sitting bowed over his plate, meticulously picking every tiny bit of skin off a drumstick. Marcus must have noticed the anxious look on my face because he leaned in and whispered, "Zachary needs time to get used to you."

"He's . . . quiet."

"Yeah, well, he's had a hard year, as you probably know."

I nodded. I had no idea what to say to someone whose mom went off the deep end like that.

"Do you live here?" he asked after a while.

"No, I live in Denver. We always come here for the summer," I said, immediately realizing my slip. There wasn't a "we" anymore. I picked up a piece of cold chicken and took a tiny bite out of it. He was still looking at me, so I added, "I mean, I do."

"Mabel told me," he said softly. "I'm sorry about your brother." He kicked at the dirt under his heel, probably unsure what else to say. Then he perked up. "Your granddad's a regular mountain man, I hear." When I looked at him, he gave me a shy half smile.

"I guess." It was nice of him to change the subject like that.

"Mabel said he did some pretty fancy stuff."

"A few first ascents."

"Of?"

"Well." I sighed, and forced a smile. "He was the first to summit Granite Peak, the highest mountain in Montana. He opened a route on Devils Tower, too."

"Oh," he said. He looked a little disappointed, as if he'd expected me to mention Mount Everest, so I added, "Blindfolded."

"One hand tied behind his back?"

"Precisely." I laughed, and Marcus grinned.

"If I had the chance, I might give climbing a try," he said, looking up at the mountains.

"Why don't you?"

"No one to teach me."

"Maybe Grandpa would. He doesn't have anyone . . ." I stalled again.

"He has you, right?"

"I don't climb," I said, bracing myself for the usual reaction. Most people were shocked that Cody McGraw's younger sister didn't scale cliff walls in her spare time.

All Marcus said was, "Ever?"

"No."

"Well, that's cool. If it's not your thing, I mean."

"I'm phobic," I replied.

He laughed, leaning back to survey the crowd. "So this is a down-home kind of shindig." He sounded like Cody doing his Willie Nelson impersonation.

"You got it, pardner," I drawled. He wasn't as hard to talk to as I'd thought he'd be, maybe because he reminded me of Cody. He seemed a little moody, but he had an easygoing way about him, and a cute smile. I decided I liked him. "Yee-haw."

"When's the square dancing begin?"

I was trying to come up with a clever comeback

when I heard a car door slam, and suddenly Penny was charging over to us, blowing tobacco smoke out her nostrils. Marcus glanced over at her. "Oh man."

"Come on, guys. I've had enough of this." Her bloodshot eyes passed over the crowd with visible dread. She didn't seem to notice me at all, which was okay because it meant I could get a look at her. Even though Mabel and my grandpa were good friends, I'd never met Penny before—she'd left the valley before I was born and had never come back. People were always gossiping about Mabel's wayward daughter, how she'd settled on a man just like her dad and that she'd be lucky if her husband drank himself to death before she did. To me she'd always been a mythic figure, but in the flesh, she wasn't so impressive. She was small and thin, and her dirty hair was clumped over haggard eyes. She tugged on Zachary's shirt until he stood up, then took his plate from him, saying, "You can eat this at home." The drumstick he'd been peeling fell on the ground to roll in the dirt.

Mabel struggled from the car, rocking it as she pulled herself out of it. It took a few tries but she finally pried herself up and started waddling toward me, her hands patting her purple muumuu. "Annie McGraw!" she exclaimed in a voice almost big enough to match the rest of her. "How long have you been sitting there?"

"Hi, Mabel," I said, contriving a smile. "How are you?"

She clapped her plump hands under her chin and shook her head. "You look more grown up every year!" I bent toward my plate as her blue eyes darted over my chest. "You're turning into a woman before our eyes!"

Marcus stifled a laugh.

I wanted to crawl under the log I was sitting on.

"Come on, Mom," Penny said. "I've got a headache."

"This is Annie." Mabel's tone flattened as she spoke to her daughter. "She'll be watching Zachary."

Penny's eyes rested on me for the first time. "Pleased to meet you," she said, though she didn't sound pleased at all. She pulled in another rough drag from her cigarette and blew it out vigorously. "Mom, I have to go. All these people—this is just too much." Her voice sounded raw and exhausted. With one hand on his shoulder, she led Zachary toward the car. As they went, she tossed her burning cigarette onto the ground, ignoring the glares of the locals around her. Littering in Jackson Hole is a capital offense.

Marcus glanced at me and quickly wrapped his napkin around the last of his burger. "I guess I'll see you," he muttered.

"Bye," I said.

He ambled away and climbed into the driver's seat of his mother's beat-up hatchback. I held up my hand to say goodbye, but his eyes were rigidly fixed through a spot on the windshield as he started the engine. Zachary and his mother slowly climbed into the backseat behind him.

Mabel looked above at the white clouds for a moment, shook her head, then shuffled herself into the car next to Marcus. Grandpa came over to stand next to me, his plate full of chicken and corn on the cob, his concerned gaze fixed on Mabel. Her tiny eyes shot at him. She waved sadly as Marcus backed out of the space. The car moved slowly out of the parking area, seeming to tow a heavy load behind it as it went.

6

Mabel had been in the house a full two minutes the next morning before she was seated at the kitchen table, biting into her first vanilla wafer. Grandpa kept a box of them on top of the fridge just for her. She was Grandpa's best friend, though I couldn't have imagined any two people less alike. While Grandpa is reclusive and athletic, Mabel is the biggest gossip in the valley, and her only exercise seems to be moving from one chair to another, which, considering her size, takes an impressive amount of effort. They became close when her husband died of liver disease only four months after my grandmother died of an aneurysm. To get through the first lonely year, Mabel would bring Grandpa supper every night. They'd been close ever since.

Grandpa put a fresh pot of coffee on to brew. "Breakfast?"

"Got any pancake dough left?" Mabel asked, sniffing the air as she patted her plump middle.

"Planned ahead." Grandpa pulled a big bowl of batter out of the fridge and set the skillet on the stove with a bang.

I was standing at the living room window looking out at Zachary, who still refused to come in. He was sitting on his purple satchel in the middle of our driveway, elbows on his knees, chin in his hands. "Is he doing okay?" I asked.

"Well, things haven't been too easy on him. But Penny's back in treatment in Pocatello. She's trying to get better." Mabel's large face took on a hard, worn look as she added, "For now."

I looked out the window again at Zachary, who was kicking at the dirt with the toe of his blue sneaker. I figured he was helping an earthworm split in two, or something mildly destructive like that.

"Why don't you go out and talk to him, Annie?" Mabel said. "See if you can make him feel at home."

As I've said, I'm not good with kids. As if stalking a wild animal, I slowly opened the screen door and eased onto the porch. "Grandpa's making pancakes. Are you hungry?" I said gently.

He didn't even look at me.

"Okay. Well, let's go onto the back porch where it's shady. Sound good?"

Slowly he picked up his purple nylon satchel and, making a wide circle around me, walked to the back of the house. I noticed more wildflowers had sprouted over Grandpa's excuse for a lawn, mostly purple lupine and Indian paintbrush. The bird feeder was swinging from the beam over the porch; a bird must have just flown away from it as we approached. The pines were making that beautiful ocean sound, sighing in the swell and fall of the wind, but Zachary seemed oblivious to it all as he sat on the porch steps. He slumped as though trying to melt into the yellow floorboards.

I sat on the porch swing and tried to be cheerful. "Do you like visiting Mabel here in Wyoming?"

He shrugged. The silence was as thick as Grandpa's pancakes.

"Maybe you'll see a bear, like I did." I hoped this would pique his interest, but he didn't even twitch. "I thought he would eat me, he got so close. He even licked me! Right here!" I showed him my arm, but he didn't look up from the floor. "So anyway, later I met this Indian who said grizzlies are called Great-Grandfather, isn't that interesting? Grandpa says I have a totem now. Or something."

He looked up and stared at the part in my hair, as if he thought looking directly at my face might cause a seizure. "Let's go inside," I finally mumbled.

He dragged his satchel into the house. It caught the living room rug and bunched it up, but he just kept going, pulling harder as if he hadn't noticed. Finally the satchel made it over the lump of carpet and he lurched into the kitchen.

Grandpa was standing at the kitchen sink, scrubbing out the skillet. When he saw Zachary, he boomed, "Want some breakfast?" He always shouts when he's trying to be friendly to children, but he only succeeds in terrifying them. Zachary cringed and rushed to Mabel's side, his eyes trailing down Grandpa's ridiculous getup.

Grandpa was wearing his frilly apron, complete with ruffles, baby blue rosebuds, and a delicate white lace trim. It had been my grandmother's, but Grandpa refused to throw it out after she died. Everything else went to Goodwill, Cody said, but the apron stayed on the hook by the stove. Grandpa turned off the tap water and boomed again, "Last chance for pancakes!"

Zachary shook his head, buried his face in Mabel's fleshy neck and whispered something to her. I heard her say, "No, honey. You stay here today. Grandma's got a lot of things to do."

I had to work hard to disguise my dread. I was being forced to spend the entire day with a kid who hated the idea as much as I did. The whole thing seemed futile, and I was angry all over again at Mom and Grandpa for making me do this. Wasn't I going through enough already?

Mabel scooted her chair back at tiny intervals and pushed herself up from the table. "Jack, thank you for those pancakes."

Grandpa took off his apron and hung it on the hook as he said, "Try not to worry. The boy'll come around."

"I hope you're right," she said. "I just wish I knew where he was spending his days. He disappears in the morning and comes back at night without a word; won't answer any of my questions."

I figured they were talking about Marcus. I didn't want to be nosy, but I couldn't help being curious about him. "Is everything okay, Mabel?"

She waved one hand in the air as she hobbled toward the door. "Marcus is a lot like his mother, is all! Won't take help from anybody!"

Grandpa picked up his truck keys and followed Mabel out the door. "Where are you going?" I asked. I'd had no idea he intended to leave me alone with Zachary.

"On the river," he said as he walked to his truck.

I followed him out and looked in the back of his pickup, but he hadn't loaded the river raft. "You're not taking the raft?"

He started his truck engine before answering, "We'll use . . . my friend's."

"Who?"

"I'll see you tonight."

"Oh. Okay." He was acting more gruff than usual, and I wondered if he was hiding something from me.

Zachary and I watched Mabel and Grandpa pull away as though they were the last lifeboats leaving a sinking ship. When the cars were gone we looked at each other. Trying to sound enthusiastic and failing miserably, I asked, "What do you feel like doing today?"

He shrugged forlornly.

"Want to listen to the radio?"

He shrugged again.

"Want to color pictures?"

Shrug.

"Want to sit on the porch swing?"

Shrug.

"How about shrugging?" I said, shrugging. "We could sit here and shrug."

He paused for a second, seeming to consider his options. Then he shrugged.

"Let's go fishing, then. We can go down to the river." I ignored Zachary's dismayed look and got the tiny fishing pole I'd used as a little girl from the closet under the loft ladder. I banged back through the screen door, handed the pole to him, picked up the tackle box and Grandpa's pole, and started down the porch steps. He slung his satchel over his shoulder and started to struggle down the steps with it. "Zachary, leave that thing on the porch. It's much too heavy to carry to the river." He gripped it more tightly. I lowered my eyebrows at him until he dropped the bag.

At least it was a beautiful day. The air was fragrant with the new buds of early summer, and the river was high, fed by melting snow from the mountains. Tiny white butterflies fluttered along the path ahead of us and shimmied between the moist leaves of the foliage as we passed. I pointed them out to Zachary, but he barely even glanced at them. At Grandpa's inlet I set the tackle box down and threaded Zachary's line through a lure.

"Have you ever fished before?" I asked him. He shook his head. I explained how to cast sideways using his whole arm for better aim. I pointed to all the jutting rocks where the trout sheltered themselves from the sun, showed him how to use weighters, and how to jerk the line to sink the hook into the fish's lip. The whole time he stared at his shoes, shrugging now and then. He finally sat down with his chin in his hands on a log nearby.

"You don't want to fish?" I finally asked him.

He shrugged.

"Well, I'm fishing." I angrily cast my line to the quicksilver of the river and let the current drag the hook downstream. It stayed there until the noonday sun shone high and hot; then I reeled in the line and picked up the tackle box and his pole. "It's lunchtime," I said, and walked up the path. I could hear the sound of his feet scraping along the trail behind me.

Lunch was so quiet I could hear Zachary chewing each of his tiny little sheepish bites. I got out the crayons from when I was a kid, and I tried to get him interested in drawing, even to the point of physically putting a red crayon in his uncooperative little hand, but he just flopped it over the paper, barely looking at what he was doing. I drew a bear cub in a pine tree and held it up for him, but his eyes wandered over it, listless, and then away. When we finally gave up on coloring, Zachary parked himself on the sofa and listened to the radio. It was tuned to a news show and can't have been too interesting for him, but I was tired of trying to reach him. I sat across from him in Grandpa's tattered easy chair, staring into space.

It's not that I don't like quiet people. I'm quiet. Quiet people are fine. Whenever I would get down about how shy I was, Mom would always laugh and say that without people like me, the blabbermouths of the world would have no audience. But this kid hadn't said a word since I'd met him.

When a car horn honked outside, Zachary jumped

off the sofa, grabbed his satchel and ran full-tilt out the door without even a wave goodbye. I followed him onto the porch and was surprised to see Marcus leaning out the window of a big blue car. "Thanks, Annie," he called as Zachary climbed in, dragging his heavy satchel after him. I was beginning to wonder what was in it. "Mabel said to tell you she'll need you to watch him next Monday, too," Marcus called.

"Sounds great," I said as he drove off. I hoped he didn't notice how artificial my smile was. I didn't think I could take even one more day with that kid. I felt bad that his mom was in an institution, but there wasn't anything I could do about it. I had my own problems. I decided I would call Mabel that night to tell her it would be best if she found someone who had more experience dealing with kids.

The sun eased behind the trees that rimmed Grandpa's yard. Soon it would sink behind the Tetons, and the long, pink dusk would begin.

I sat on the porch and listened to the birds in the pines chirping their afternoon song. A couple of ravens were having an argument, probably fighting over a smelly carcass somewhere. Their angry caws interrupted the other birds, who paused in their song to eavesdrop. When the ravens quieted, the smaller birds resumed, beginning with a tentative question from a brave little chickadee.

I was about to go back in when I heard car tires crushing the pine needles in the driveway. I expected it to be Grandpa, but it was Marcus again, alone in his beat-up blue car. I sat back down on the steps and waited while he got out and walked to the porch, stopping just short of the stairs. "Hi again."

I swallowed hard and squeaked, "Hi." I tried to smile, but it felt more like a grimace. He made me so thrillingly nervous.

"I just dropped Zachary off at Mabel's. He was a little upset."

My stomach tied itself into a slipknot. "About what?"

"He said you didn't talk to him all day."

"I tried! He's just so quiet. I finally decided to leave him to himself." Marcus looked at me defensively. I felt puny. "I'm sorry. I guess I'm not a very good babysitter."

"Not on the first day, anyway." I must have looked hurt because he waved away his words and sat next to me on the porch. "Look, I know he's not the easiest kid right now. Especially with people he doesn't know."

"I know how he feels," I said, then I realized I'd revealed more than I'd wanted to.

Marcus studied me a moment, then nodded. "Yeah, you seem a little shy, too."

"I was thinking he would do better with someone more outgoing."

"You're thinking of quitting?"

"I just don't think it's working."

He flashed me a look of urgency. "Don't quit. He'd feel rejected, and that isn't what he needs right now."

"I'm just . . . Now isn't a good time for me to be dealing with . . ."

"Annie, he's a great kid, he's just freaked out lately. Please, try one more day."

Maybe it was the way he said my name, or the intense way he was looking at me. It could have been that the way he cared so much about his little brother reminded me of how Cody used to be with me. Whatever it was, in that moment I couldn't say no. "I'll give it another try."

"Okay. Thanks." He gave me a halting grin.

I smiled, this time for real. I wasn't thrilled about Zachary, but I was happy to do something for Marcus.

He started to walk to his car, but stopped short and turned back to me. "You know, Zach and I are going to

Yellowstone on Sunday. Maybe . . . I don't know." His gaze scattered over the pine needles on the ground, but then trained on me. "Maybe you could come? That might help him get used to you?"

I was so stunned that I hardly noticed my jaw dropping. Maybe I should have been happy, but the idea made me anxious. I could barely speak in complete sentences around Marcus. How could I spend a whole day with him? "D-do you think it would help?"

"Sure. You could show us around." He put one hand in his jeans pocket and looked at me from under his heavy dark bangs. He was so cute.

"Okay." I felt myself flushing and tried furiously to make it go away, but my cheeks only colored more.

"I'll pick you up at ten?"

"Sounds good."

He looked at me for a few seconds, a grin spreading over his face as though something made him want to bubble over with laughter. I caught the mood and smiled back.

He got into his rusty car and drove off, and I stood on the porch watching him go, wondering whether I'd just been asked out on a date.

7

After nightfall Grandpa still wasn't home. A weird kind of nervous high from the Marcus interaction sent me pacing through the cabin, looking for something to occupy myself. Grandpa had no TV, and I had run out of library books to read, so I decided to look through Grandma's photo album. I didn't look through it often—most of the pictures were of people I had never met, relatives in Chicago who were mostly dead already. But now I studied the smiles and frowns, looking for traces of Cody, of me.

At the back was my favorite picture. It showed my mother as a teenager, standing between my grandmother and Grandpa's mother. Mom looked like a regular kid, wearing jeans and a T-shirt, her curly brown hair pulled back in a ponytail. Both my grandmother and my great-grandmother were big and round; their hair was pulled into buns. Grandma's hair was streaked with gray, but her face was still young, and her smile was peaceful. My great-grandmother looked stern as she squinted bravely into the camera, her hair a shocking white. Grandpa resembled her, with his severe pale eyes and serious expression.

I flipped to another photo of my grandmother as a young woman, standing under a tree in a cap and gown. Underneath it was written: *Anna Beth, College Graduation.* I could see from the picture that my name wasn't all I'd inherited from her. She had straight, coarse hair like mine, and a small mouth with thin lips. There were familiar traces—in the way our smiles didn't quite manage to turn completely upward, in the way our wide eyes exuded innocence. She even stood with her hands clasped behind her back, which is almost always how I pose for photos—I never know what to do with my arms. I stared at her picture and tried hard to remember her, but my only memory was of fragrant gray hair against my cheek as she hugged me goodbye.

I closed the album before I got to the newer pictures, the ones I took, first those with my Instamatic, and then the professional-looking ones with my Nikon. I didn't want to remember the Annie who got up before daybreak to get a shot of the owl I kept hearing at night. Everything seemed dark and underexposed with Cody gone, even my perfect photos.

I bent down to put the album back in the cherry-wood hutch, but something in the back kept it from sliding in. I reached in to scoot it out of the way and pulled out a bunch of dusty, yellowed papers, tied together with a strip of calico. I opened the bundle to find letters, three of them, two written in sloping, graceful handwriting, the other in Grandpa's small, square characters. I read the first page, my heart galloping as I realized what I'd found.

> Dear Jack,
>   I've taken Amanda and I've gone back to Chicago. I need time to think. Please don't write or call. I'll contact you when I have my thoughts composed.

I know you deserve an explanation, and all I can say is that I feel so alone here I can barely stand it. You won't talk to me. Your parents barely say anything to anyone. I feel trapped in this horrible cabin, and I feel if I don't leave I might lose my mind. If there were any other way, believe me, I would try it.

I'm sorry, Jack.
Yours,
Ann

I read it again, but the meaning was unmistakable. Grandma had left Grandpa? Mom had always talked about her parents' marriage as if it had been perfect. Grandpa was utterly devoted; Grandma babied him. I should have known the image Mom had created for me and Cody was too glossy.

I flipped through the envelopes and looked at the postmarks. They spanned November through January the year after my mother was born. Grandma and Grandpa would have been married about two years. I opened the first letter again and ran my fingers over the ink. I shouldn't read them, I knew it. That would be an invasion of privacy. But I needed to know the rest of the story. Why did Grandma come back to him?

I read them in order, over and over, until I practically had them memorized.

November 25
Jack,

I want you to stop calling me. You wouldn't talk to me for months, and now suddenly you have loads of things you want to say? Now it's me who doesn't want to talk.

Just put yourself in my shoes for a minute, if you're capable of doing so. You move away from everything you know, from a busy, bustling city where your friends and family live, and you're in the middle of nowhere. There is no one to talk to. The silence of those surrounding you is impenetrable. Your parents-in-law tiptoe around you like you're a communist spy. The snow is so deep that on some days you can't leave the cabin, so you have nowhere to go to be alone. No privacy at all. You have a baby to care for, and you're absolutely terrified about her future in such a desolate place. You wouldn't be melancholy? You wouldn't be in shock? Then add to that, your spouse, the one person you should be able to turn to, ignores you, behaves as if you were a madwoman for feeling afraid. And finally, when you're at your darkest hour, crying uncontrollably, he leaves the room. Without a word of comfort or concern. He just leaves you there, alone.

I don't think you love me. If you loved me, you would have asked me what was wrong. You would have put your arms around me. You would have tried to help me. So I left, Jack. Of course I left you. What else could I have done?

I want you to keep away. I don't want to talk to you or hear from you. Just stay away from me.

Ann

January 10
Annie,

I had a restless feeling when I woke up. I strapped on my snowshoes and walked into the forest early. The air was crisp, the kind of cold that stings your eyes. A bitter day seems about right, though, because you're not here.

Everything was still. A day when the breeze settles soon after dawn because it's so cold. I found a moose standing in the sun. I *saw a lot of snowshoe hare tracks. Even ran across mountain lion tracks near a creek so small no one's bothered to name it. That restless feeling didn't go away, though.*

So I turned uphill and started into the mountains. It was near midday and I kept on looking. Kept getting my snowshoes caught on fallen trees, roots of trees, branches. Ran across a big aspen that was scratched up by a bear. Saw a hawk resting near the top of a lodgepole pine. Ran across a pure white ermine. He stopped when he saw me. His black eyes fixed on my eyes. Seemed to be asking if he could trust me. Reminded me of the way you used to look at me.

Made the restless feeling worse.

It was getting dark. I thought about going on all night, snagging myself on twigs and branches. Coming across animals. Looking at them. Letting them get a good look at me. It was no use. My restless feeling would've stayed with me if I'd walked all the way to Alaska. Or Chicago.

It won't ever go away, Annie. This feeling that drives me into the wilderness won't ever leave me. Not as long as you're away.

I love you. Please come home.

Jack

It was nearly bedtime when I tied the calico strip around the letters and tucked them back in the cabinet. Grandpa still wasn't home.

I crawled up to my cot and lay in the dark, listening to the night sounds. I had more questions about their life together than I'd ever had. I knew one thing for sure, though. Grandpa had been far from the perfect husband, and Grandma had seen him the same way I did: cold and unyielding. Unreachable.

I felt vindicated, but one thing nagged at me. I'd never seen Grandpa write anything other than a grocery list. Whenever he expressed any emotion, it embarrassed him. But his letter was beautiful.

I closed my eyes, letting sleep settle on me, thinking about Grandpa wandering through the forest, finding bear sign on an aspen, missing his wife.

8

I am in the forest where the light doesn't change. Dream forest. I am walking through a meadow of blue morning glories. The sunlight slants at a permanent angle, soaking through the treetops to land dappled on the soft forest floor. The breeze whispers through the branches above, spirals downward and wraps around me like a shroud. I kneel to pick the tender flowers.

When I stand up, all the trees are dead charcoal slabs jutting through fine black dust. Everything burned. Everything gone.

I smell the grizzly in the air and know I have to follow. I have to find him quickly.

I run through the blackened forest, coals hot on my feet, my throat burning. My breath is urgent and choked, but I know he is here somewhere.

I reach a clearing draped in cruel shadows. I drop to my knees because they are waiting for me.

The grizzly is at the edge of the charred trees, snout pointed to someone standing at the center of the clearing.

I gasp.

Cody. He's standing with his back to me, his hands in his pockets, wearing that ugly orange vest he seemed to live in.

He's been waiting for me to find him, and I realize I'm terribly, horribly late. Too late. I suck in dry air and it makes me choke. Black ashes fall from my eyes to join the ashes on the blackened ground.

"When are you coming home?" My voice is minuscule, barely able to pierce the ashes to reach him. "Cody?"

My brother turns to look at me.

His eyes are glassy, his skin is stiff and waxen, his once beautiful face deflated and inert.

The bear licks my arm, nudges me toward him.

"No," I say.

Cody smiles at me, his stiff lips stretching over yellowed teeth. His voice becomes the stale wind moving like a razor through the forest, carrying the smell of smoke and death. His words fall like whispers of ashes.

"Help me."

+ + +

I didn't know where I was or that I was screaming until the light in the loft came on and I saw Grandpa rush up the ladder, out of breath. "What is it?"

"I'm okay." I hid my shaking hands in my hair, but I

couldn't hide my trembling, so I lay back down and pulled the covers up to my chin.

"Thought you had a bat in here."

"Just a dream." I tried to sound normal but my voice came out small.

He stood at the foot of my bed, his gaze wandering over the pattern of the pink quilt on my knees. Even in the dim light, Grandpa's eyes were the icy blue of a mountain glacier. Finally, he mumbled, "Want to . . . talk?" He cleared his throat, then added, "Muffin?"

He hadn't called me that in years. When I was Muffin, Cody was just starting to climb. Those were the days of Chinese checkers, when we used to drag Grandpa to the kitchen table to play just one more game. He would act like he hated every minute, but he always let me win, and I would kiss him good night before following Cody up the ladder to the loft, so tired because he'd let us stay up late again.

Now all I had left of Cody were nightmares, and I didn't want to be alone in the dark. I started to say something but I didn't know what I needed Grandpa to do. I wanted things to be like when Cody and I were little, but it could never be like that again.

I looked at him, trying to reconcile this man with the beautiful letter he'd written for my grandmother so long ago. I couldn't. He seemed so cold, so cheerless. Even when I was Muffin. I would throw my arms around his neck and nuzzle my little face in his cheek, but he always accepted my kisses so passively.

Grandpa finally got up and muttered, "Get some sleep." He crawled down the ladder and was gone.

I lay there, watching the shadows on the ceiling, concentrating on the mystery in my grandparents' letters so I wouldn't have to remember the blackened forest. I didn't want to think about what that awful nightmare could mean.

9

The morning light peered at me sideways through the windowpane. I lay in bed letting the sun itch my face until Grandpa came up the ladder and clamped a hand on my shoulder. "We're taking a hike today."

We started early, heading southwest into the mountains where the granite of the Tetons pokes through the red dirt on the trails. The pines there were young, their trunks skinny and straight, green with juicy wood and soft needles. It had been a dry winter that year, so the grass was sparse and flaccid, dotted here and there by weak wildflowers. Plants in the mountains always rely on snowmelt for their water, and if winter is kind to the animals by falling mild and soft, then spring is a cruel time for the vegetation that comes after the thaw. Somehow, though, the wildflowers bloom every year.

We climbed high to where the trail was steep and jagged. The sharp sun made my eyelids feel heavy, especially where the sheltering trees yielded to a rock field that rose far up the mountainside, clear into the sapphire sky. Glacial water trickled between the chunks of granite, seeping onto the trail to make thick, slimy mud. It was so slippery I had to walk with my arms extended to keep my balance. I could hear an immense waterfall somewhere up ahead, and I knew that must be where Grandpa was leading me.

The path eased into a slight incline, and we were in the shade of the trees again. We'd climbed so high there was still snow on the ground, even in the warmth of June. Abruptly, the trail petered out at a wide cliff ledge.

Grandpa, fearless, walked to the rim of the rock and looked into the canyon. A column of water tumbled down the cliff to Grandpa's left, curving away from the mountain, so I couldn't see its top. Bright cliffs lined the bed of the stream that flowed from these falls. The darkness where we stood made the granite across the chasm seem brighter still, faraway rock glowing silver in the sunlight. The air was heavy and clung to the tree branches around us, wet greens sagging with the weight of mist. It was cold here in this dark dampness. If I craned my neck to the right I could glimpse the valley floor where the elk grazed along Flat Creek. We'd climbed high.

Grandpa was still for a long time, and I stood well behind him, feeling the deafening force of the water vibrate through the air. "Dad called these Shadow Falls," he finally said, "because the way the canyon is, sunlight never gets to it. Good name, but the guidebooks call it something else." He had to yell to be heard over the water, and every word seemed to bend him over a little. "Haven't been, since Dad died. Reminds me too much. Now I got to find places that don't remind me of, well . . ." He turned away to look into the plummet.

I just stood there, staring at his angular profile. That was the most I'd heard him speak in a long time, but he still couldn't bring himself to mention Cody.

Grandpa waved me forward. "Take a look."

I moved toward the lip of the shelf, but the canyon seemed like an evil force waiting to suck me down to my death. A picture sparked in my mind of my body lying broken and bleeding at the end of a fall. *Like Gary. Like Cody.* My head swam and my legs wobbled. Heart pounding, I backed away so quickly I almost tripped.

I leaned on a boulder and spread my palms, reassuring myself that everything around me was solid, that I couldn't fall in.

Grandpa didn't notice my vertigo. He was bent over his pack, rooting through it. I thought he was looking for some water or a snack, but he pulled out a climbing harness and spread it on the ground.

"What are you doing?" I asked, incredulous. Did he actually imagine he was going to leave me behind again to go climbing?

He cocked his head toward the rock wall looming above us. "That's an easy wall. I thought maybe you could try it, if you want to." He bent back down and started pulling out a length of rope. It was the same faded purple coil he'd taken on so many climbing trips with Cody, the same rope I'd once carried, hoping they'd finally let me climb with them. They never did.

Now that Cody was gone, suddenly I was allowed to climb? I was finally good enough? I thought again about what Grandpa had said. *There's McGraw blood in there somewhere.* "How can you even think of climbing again?" I asked him.

"What do you mean?" He blinked at me, completely dumbfounded.

I stared back at him, the words churning in my mind. *How can you want to climb after the way Cody died? Is climbing more important to you than your own grandchildren? Does anything affect you?* These thoughts I couldn't speak; instead, a harsh laugh tumbled out. "I'm not climbing," I said.

"You always wanted to." He smiled and picked up the rope, held it toward me. "Now's your chance."

I dropped my eyes to his shoes, forcing words through the straight line of my mouth. "I don't want to anymore."

"You're a McGraw!"

I stood there, unsure whether to explode or cry, letting the feelings cancel each other out. I was left with a confused rage that allowed only a steady glare at him, a stony silence.

"Try it, Annie." Grandpa grabbed my hand, but I jerked away. "No way you'll fall." He held up the harness to show me. "I'll protect you."

"Like you protected Cody?" I said it before I even knew I'd thought it.

"What?"

Maybe he hadn't heard me over the falls, or maybe he just couldn't believe what I'd said. I backtracked, suddenly unsure of what I felt. "I'll never climb, okay?" I said; and again so there could be no doubt: "I will never climb."

He stared at me, utterly confused and hurt. I didn't care. Grandpa had pushed Cody into deadly altitudes. He wasn't going to push me.

He shook his head and knelt down to stuff the rope and harness back into his pack, his movements halting, as if even his joints had been injured by my rejection.

I raised my face to the sky and spied an eagle spiraling through the air currents that blew among the cold rocks on the mountainside. It flew in and out of the sunshine, first glowing in the full light of noon, then swooping back under the shadow of a little white cloud, then into the light again. Back and forth, light and dark, endless.

Grandpa tugged on the strap of my backpack. "Darla's expecting us soon anyway," he mumbled.

This was news to me. "Who?" I planted my feet, refusing to move.

"Darla," he said over his shoulder. "Moved here this spring. Bought Ed Greeley's place." He turned his back on me and started down the trail.

It was unusual for Grandpa to go over to other people's houses, and unheard of for him to make friends with a newcomer to the valley. I was curious, but still too angry to talk, so I followed him in silence.

Grandpa led me the way we'd come. I fixed my eyes on his back, and for the first time noticed how curved it had become, how stiff his gait. I hated how old he was getting.

Going downhill was faster, but I felt the pull in my knees. I was focusing on my footsteps, trudging in time with the mean beating of my heart, when I nearly fell over Grandpa. With no warning at all he'd stooped to looked at something in the trail. "Bear track," he muttered, buckling his brow. "Fresh." He traced with his finger until I saw where claws had scratched the hard clay and a huge pad had pressed into the dust.

"Black, or grizzly?"

He shook his head, unsure.

I wiped the sweat from my eyes with trembling fingers. It's never good to run into a black bear, but grizzlies are worse. Much worse. I remembered the bear on the river, its breath on me, its tender tongue gliding along my skin, tasting me. I didn't want to believe it was the same animal, but I knew it could be. Grizzlies can range dozens of miles in a single day, and though they tend to claim an area as their territory, they've been known to move.

Under the high angle of the hot sun, I shivered.

The truth is, I'd been lucky the bear hadn't mauled me that morning. Most people who surprise a grizzly like that are fortunate to end up in the hospital instead of the morgue. Every year I read about a grizzly attack in the papers. One photographer from New Jersey lost an eye and the ability to speak because he thought he could get a close-up of a cub. Not exactly a genius to begin with, but he didn't deserve brain damage. A forest ranger got mauled when he surprised a bear on his morning jog. He got one hundred and eighty stitches and a whole lot of blood transfusions. The worst story, though, was about a woman who was camping with her friends. She didn't know you shouldn't sleep in clothes you cook in, and late at night, when the whole camp was asleep, a grizzly tore through her tent in search of the food scent. He dragged her away in her sleeping bag. Every mile or so he would stop to maul her, and then he would drag her farther into the woods. The authorities didn't have any trouble finding her remains the next day because the trail was pretty clear—a finger here, a piece of scalp there. When they found the bear they killed it.

I looked down the path. There were tracks as far as I could see. I tried to keep my voice even as I asked, "Was he following us up the mountain?"

"Maybe. At a distance."

"Was he hunting us?"

He turned to look at me sternly over his shoulder. "Come on," he said, and took off at a fast pace.

We went down the switchbacks cautiously but quickly. At each bend I hoped the tracks would end, but they didn't. As far as I could see the trail, I could see faint paw prints. I remembered the bear in my awful nightmare and tried to blink the image away.

We finally reached the muddy rock field, and again Grandpa stooped to examine the trail. I didn't have to know anything about tracking to see the perfect imprint of a huge bear paw in the mud. It was a grizzly. No doubt about it. The claws were several inches long, and I could have fit both my feet into the bowl left by the bear's enormous heel pad. I swallowed hard.

"He's big." Grandpa wiped his forehead with his bandanna as he scanned the trees around us.

Great-Grandfather is watching you, the old man had said. The fibers of my dreams wove through the forest air. I heard the call of a magpie, and it sounded like a warning that we were being watched.

Grandpa picked up a couple of rocks and told me to do the same. "Don't want to surprise him." We descended the rest of the way to the valley floor, slapping rocks together, making as much noise as we could. We paused here and there to look around, but there was no bear sign—other than ghosts of paw prints overlapping ours—for miles.

The tracks disappeared as soon as the trail leveled onto the valley floor. Grandpa visibly relaxed as we curved to the south, out of the forest and through fields of wildflowers, where the visibility was better. No bear in sight.

Still, I could feel the grizzly in the forest behind us. Waiting.

10

A half hour of winding paths brought us to a tiny cabin tucked into a grove of aspens. Grandpa pulled a short comb out of his pants pocket and ran it over his white hair. I looked at him askance. I'd never known him to comb his hair more than once a day. He knocked on the door but walked right in, calling, "Ahoy!"

"Ahoy!" A sprightly, middle-aged woman rushed from the kitchen. She reminded me of a wren fluttering over to us as she shook her hair out of her gray eyes. Holding out her hand to me, she smiled warmly and said, "Anna Beth. It's very nice to meet you." Her voice was crisp, decidedly English. She rushed back to the kitchen, calling over her shoulder, "Sit. I was just putting together a tray."

The living room was nicely arranged with elegant furniture of antique hardwood. We sat on a winged sofa of deep navy blue. The walls, the usual Wyoming brown log, were hung with dozens of photographs, all framed in ornate pewter. One of the pictures showed a very handsome young man with black hair and a luminous smile. He had Darla's gray eyes and delicate skin.

"Nice place, right?" Grandpa asked eagerly, as if he needed my approval.

"Very Emily Brontë," I muttered, giving him a curious look. He was acting weirdly nervous.

Darla, still wearing her apron, carried in a beaten silver tray laden with sandwiches, some sort of berry tart, cheese slices, English tea biscuits, and grapes. I was starved from the long hike, and my mouth watered.

"Have what you like, dear." She sat down in the chair and tucked her legs underneath her. Grandpa helped himself to a plateful of food and I followed suit, too hungry to be shy.

"How was your hike?" Darla asked, sipping her tea.

Grandpa said, "Saw grizzly tracks."

She leaned forward. "My, Anna, you've had quite a week for bears, haven't you?"

I nodded, wondering when Grandpa would have told her about the bear on the river. Darla was new to the valley, and it usually took Grandpa a couple of years to warm up to someone. Even this small intimacy seemed pretty extreme for him.

"Followed us up the canyon," Grandpa added.

"Really? But you never saw him once?"

Grandpa shook his head, took a bite of a cucumber sandwich and washed it down with some tea.

"I was thinking, I should like to see that Native American man you met, Jack. There's a good chance I know him." Another thing he'd told her.

"Darla's an anthropologist," Grandpa told me proudly. He seemed eager for me to like Darla. I was beginning to wonder what their relationship was. The way they looked at each other, their eyes shining, cheeks polished pink, they were like two kids on their first date. But I'd never known Grandpa to take any interest in women, not after Grandma. This whole thing was making me suspicious. "Darla studies the nations in the area," Grandpa added.

Darla looked at me expectantly, a cheery smile on her face. Obviously, it was my turn to speak.

"Um . . . is that why you came to the States?" I asked through a mouthful of grapes.

"Goodness, no! The only thing that could take me away from my dear old England was a handsome man!"

Grandpa giggled. He actually giggled, like a schoolgirl. The man was positively giddy. I glanced at Darla, who seemed to concentrate purposefully on the tea she was sipping. Grandpa caught my eye and reeled himself in, forcing the usual stoic expression back on his face.

I looked over at the pictures on the wall, and Darla followed my gaze. "You're admiring my photographs, I see. Bion was my son."

Was. I'd come to notice things like that. Some time must have passed since he died because she didn't stumble on his name. I hadn't gotten to that point. Still, I could see real grief pinching her face as she solemnly handed me a picture of the handsome young man in a graduation cap. He was entwined in the arms of a younger Darla. She smiled sadly and said, "I think that's my favorite picture. He looks so happy there."

I didn't want to take the chance of upsetting her by asking what happened to him, even though it was what I most wanted to know. Instead I asked, "So his father was American?"

"British. He was an archaeologist, and very interested in the Shoshone of central Wyoming. I was foolish enough to quit medical school to follow him here. I was terribly bored, living in a rin-tin shack on the reservation. After I stopped feeling sorry for myself, I started making friends with the women and learned how unpopular my husband was." Her expression flickered with an old frustration. "He never bothered to consult the people his archaeological dig pertained to, and had little regard for their feelings about his tearing through their cemeteries."

I remembered a news program I'd seen about this. "I thought they didn't let people do that."

"Oh, this was long before they finally got fed up and started using legal means to defend themselves. At any rate, I became good friends with some of the women, and they trusted me enough to share their way of life with me. Soon, with the tribe's unusually generous consent, I was publishing as many papers as Winston was, about traditional healing techniques, both herbal and spiritual."

I searched her wall for a picture of the archaeologist, but she seemed to read my mind. "You won't find his photo up there. We divorced quite some time ago. He hadn't bargained on a woman who could think as well as cook." She poured herself another cup of tea and curled further into her chair. "Men of your grandfather's generation still have some attitudes to recover from." She narrowed her eyes at Grandpa.

I looked at him and thought of all the times he'd refused to bring me up the mountain. He was old-fashioned—always holding doors for me, and always holding me back. I'd known this on a deep level, but no one in my family ever talked about it. That Darla was bringing it up so matter-of-factly made me feel liberated. "Yeah. I know what you mean," I said.

"Of course, Anna. I have a feeling you've had your own trials in this area," Darla said, looking pointedly at Grandpa.

"I've always treated Annie the same as anyone else," Grandpa insisted.

I rolled my eyes.

Darla laughed. "I'm not sure Anna would agree with you, Jack."

"Come on, Annie. You know I treated you just like I did Cody."

"Whatever you say, Grandpa."

"What? There were no special favors for either of you!"

"Oh yeah? You started teaching Cody to climb when he was ten!" I hadn't possessed the courage to bring this up in years, but with Darla around, I suddenly felt I had an ally. "I was twelve and you still refused to teach me!"

Darla's jaw dropped. "Is this true, Jack?"

"You just told me you never want to climb!" he exclaimed in outrage.

"That's not the point. Until now you wouldn't have let me anyway."

"Jack?" Darla's eyebrows cinched. She looked like a schoolteacher upbraiding a student.

Grandpa looked from her to me as though he were cornered in a street fight. "She wasn't ready."

"I could do twenty pull-ups."

"Twenty?" Darla exclaimed. "I don't think I've ever managed a single one!"

Grandpa looked at the floor. "She had trouble learning the knots."

After giving Grandpa a long, stern look, she turned to me. "What do you think, Anna? Should we string him up?"

"I'll tie the noose."

Darla laughed out loud. I decided I really liked her, especially now that she'd sided with me against Grandpa.

He just shook his head, seeming totally bewildered by the conversation. I was glad. After fifteen years of feeling brushed aside, it was nice to knock Grandpa off balance for a change.

Darla patted Grandpa's knee and said, "Against all evidence, I am operating under the belief that men are worth saving from themselves." Grandpa blushed.

"But Anna, you shouldn't have to deal with so much pigheadedness among your peers. Young men these days seem to be making real strides."

I thought about Marcus and wondered if this was true.

"Now, I would love to hear all about you, Anna," Darla gushed. "Your grandfather has shown me some of your photography. You're really fantastic, you know that? You should start showing your work professionally!"

"Oh, I don't know."

"I know the owner of a gallery in Jackson. I could introduce you."

"I'm not really into it anymore."

She stopped for a moment to study me. "Why is that?"

"I just . . ." What could I tell her? That after Cody died, suddenly my camera weighed five hundred pounds? That it's impossible to be a photographer when the whole world seems gray? "I got bored with it," I finally said.

"Bored?" Her eyes moved over me skeptically. I shifted uneasily in my seat until Grandpa jumped in, saying, "You two have something in common. Annie is quite a reader, too."

"And a brilliant student, you've told me. What's your favorite subject?"

"Sarcasm," I said. She laughed warmly, so I decided to give her a straight answer. "English."

"And after high school, have you any plans?"

"College, I suppose."

"Good for you. Don't you make the same mistake I did and let a man run off with your heart and your education." Again, the dark look flickered over her. "I could have been a physician, but I settled for nursing to make Winston happy. It was the biggest mistake of my life. There's plenty of time for love after college." She looked wistfully out the windows, and the conversation waned, each of us in our own thoughts, until Darla suddenly said, "Your bear has me wondering, Anna."

"You mean Smokey?" I quipped, but walking through the woods scared of having the flesh ripped from my bones had not made me feel that this was *my* bear at all.

Darla sprang from her chair and went to an over-stuffed bookcase. She pulled out a tattered text and started thumbing through the pages. "I seem to remember reading something about a myth. . . ." She sat back down, muttering to herself. Grandpa leaned back, rubbing his eyes. I relaxed into the sofa, heavy from Darla's sandwiches and warm tea. Through the window I could see the sky already turning violet. I hoped we wouldn't have to walk home through the dark forest where my bear lived.

"Ah! Here it is. It's a Nez Percé legend." She squinted at the page as she read aloud: "A young boy became separated from his family in the mountains during a bitterly cold winter. Shedding many tears, he wandered through the snow calling the names of those in his tribe. Only the animals of the forest heard him. They called a council to discuss the problem of this young boy, who would surely not survive the winter alone.

" 'I cannot help him. My den is too small,' said Fox.

" 'He cannot live where I live. It is too wet,' said Beaver.

" 'I will take him,' said Grizzly Bear, who had lost her cub and was lonely.

"So in a large, warm den, against the furry belly of the great bear, the boy slept, safe and protected.

"In the spring Grizzly said to the boy, 'Come with me,' and she led him over the Bitterroot Mountains, where they spent their summer eating berries and pine nuts and ptarmigan. As winter drew near, they returned to their warm den and slept again through the frigid months.

"The boy stayed with Grizzly until one day his people found him and brought him back to live in the village. He showed his family the path over the Bitterroot Mountains where they found their pine nuts and berries. One summer, the boy disappeared again into the valley of the Grizzly. Some said the bear killed him because he showed his people her hiding place. Some said that he returned to the den of the Great Bear to sleep through the winter, for now the boy was more bear than Nez Percé."

Darla closed the book, her eyes darting at me and away quickly, but not before registering the look on my face. She seemed embarrassed. "I didn't think how . . . close to home that legend was."

I stirred my tea emphatically until I could say, "Got one in there about unicorns?" But my mouth was dry, and I could tell by the way she was looking at me that Darla knew I was pretending.

She seemed to be trying to cover for me as she said, too cheerfully, "I'm just going to carry these dishes into the kitchen." Grandpa looked at me uncomfortably for a second, but then followed Darla out of the room.

I stepped onto the porch to get ahold of myself.

That legend plunged me backward into the crazy hope I'd had for weeks after the phone call. I'd insanely imagine Cody under the avalanche in an ice cave, eating snow for moisture, chewing on jerky he miraculously had in his coat. I was sure he was waiting to be rescued, that the recovery crews would find him, cold but intact. After a week or so I started making deals. Knowing he couldn't last so long without some damage, I'd think I could live with it if he came back with a foot missing from frostbite, or maybe the tip of his nose (it's amazing what plastic surgeons can do these days). Even when we had the funeral—an outrageous, futile ceremony at the foot of an empty grave—I still wouldn't give up. I thought that even if he had to spend his life in a wheelchair, I'd find a way to get him through it. I would take care of him. I would feed him through a straw if I had to. I begged God for him to just be alive up there, somewhere under the ice. He could have amnesia or brain damage or be a quadriplegic or anything, anything. Just not dead.

Teams of searchers looked for weeks, but finally gave up after concluding that all the climbers must have been pushed into a crevasse. Recovery of any remains was impossible, they said.

But a bear could help him. A bear could keep Cody warm enough to last forever, even under the ice. If that Indian legend were true, my brother could just be sleeping, safe and alive, in the arms of a grizzly.

11

Do you remember our last climb with Gary? Remember that brown bear? We're walking up that ridge, and he's far away, down in a deep valley, pacing back and forth, kicking up his front legs like he's goose-stepping. Gary says very pensively, "I wonder what he's thinking." You laugh and slap the back of his head. Gary was always saying goofy things like that.

I can picture the whole thing. It's late August. You and I are headed out to Denver next week, and you want to get one more climb in. You and Grandpa have been itching to get yourselves up Teewinot, but I want to come along and that means you have to do something quicker and easier. So we hike up those hellish switchbacks to Lake Solitude. Nine miles from the trailhead. It's a tough hike, but I'm equal to it.

I'm determined that today I will climb a wall with you, even if it kills me. I insist on carrying up the rope because at twelve years old I'm naive enough to believe that doing so entitles me to use it. It's heavy, too, grooving deep into my shoulder. Coils and coils of it are draped over my chest, but I won't let Grandpa take it away from me.

Gary is walking behind me singing, "Sunshine on my shoulders makes me happy," over and over because those are the only words he knows from that song. After about the hundredth time you chime in, "Gary shutting up makes me happy." Gary snorts at that one. And I'm so happy because I'm sure this is the day Grandpa is finally going to let me come up with you. My arms are rock hard and carved into every discrete muscle. I can do twenty pull-ups and fifty push-ups without even trying. There's no way Grandpa can say I'm not ready. I am ready, even if I'm scared. I'm ready.

Finally we make it to Solitude, a small glacial lake that reflects the profile of the Tetons on its glassy surface. We're high up; the trees are already starting to look a little shorter. And all around us are sheets of granite, fields of boulders. You look at that sweeping mass of stone jutting into the sky, and you lick your lips like it's a pile of flapjacks.

The wind smells of snow, and I can tell by the sting of it that it has just been hurtling itself over the glaciers above us. I close my eyes and hear the whispers of the pines and the wooden creaking of their trunks. I drink practically my whole water bottle. I can feel my entire body singing with the exertion of getting here, and I'm not even afraid of the long hike back home. I am strong.

You start sorting out the ropes while Grandpa hands out tuna fish sandwiches. He has that stupid mustache, remember it? It makes him look ten years older, and he seems to always have crumbs sticking to it. If I remember right, it will be fall before he finally figures out he looks ridiculous. That must be right before Gary dies.

You're fitting yourself with your climbing harness when I see Gary walk right up behind you and start singing into your ear, "Sunshine on my shoulders—"

"I swear to God, you freak!" you yell, laughing.

I see Grandpa smirking as he chalks his fingers, so I feel it's a good time to ask. "Can I go up today?"

Everyone stops what they're doing and looks at me. You seem embarrassed as you say, "I didn't know you wanted to today, Annie."

I glare at you. I can't believe you could undermine me like this. Part of me wants to scream at you that you're nothing but a traitor, but I don't want to blow my chances, so I simply say, "Of course I do, Cody. You know I do."

You look at your hands as if your gloves are taking all your concentration.

Grandpa looks me up and down and says, "We only have three harnesses, Muffin."

"Tie one out of rope then, like you used to do before they made harnesses."

Gary nods in that dopey way he had and says, "Sure, Annie can use mine and I'll tie myself in."

Grandpa gives Gary a look, then says, "Muffin, I know you want to, but . . ."

I look at him eagerly, thinking I can turn his mind with my wide, hopeful eyes.

You tilt your head to one side and look plaintively at Grandpa. He looks at you. Then Grandpa says, "It's not a good day to start, Annie."

"Don't say that again!"

"This wall is too difficult."

"Then let's go back down the trail to an easier place!"

"Annie," you say, "Grandpa's got a move he wants to show me up there."

"What about me?" I look at all of you. You and Grandpa look back, blue eyes ganging up on me, stern and unmoved. Only Gary seems troubled. He looks down at his feet, his face drooping. "You're going to leave me here?" I ask unsteadily. "Again?"

"You have your camera." You come up to me and drape one heavy arm over my shoulder as if to say,

Come on, sport! Take one for the team. Be a pal! I wish I could punch you, I'm so mad, but I can't. You're my big brother, my hero. Instead I slip from under your arm and drag myself over to sit on a log.

Gary throws his harness back into his pack and says, "You know, I'm thinking a nice nap down here might be a good break, and you fools can poop yourselves out climbing. Then me and Annie'll be fresh for the hike down and you guys can drag your sorry asses on the trail behind you." Gary pulls his T-shirt off and starts kicking his way into the frigid, frigid water of Lake Solitude. When he's up to his belly he screams, "Holy cannoli, it's cold!" He makes a walrus face at me and shakes his jowls. "Bludda bludda bludda!" I'm miserable, but the guy is making an ass of himself to try to cheer me up, so I give him half a grin.

You and Grandpa take this as your cue and you slip away, carrying your harnesses and ropes with you as you walk around the lake and up into the crook of the mountains.

Two months later Gary's life ends with a thirty-foot fall onto the granite of Cloudveil Dome.

I never want to climb again.

12

"Don't let him take any drugs," Grandpa said as he washed the breakfast dishes, wearing that ridiculous frilly apron. From behind he looked like Julia Child with a butch haircut. He certainly sounded like a worried old woman. "You can call me from anywhere and I'll come get you."

"If I'm sold into slavery, I'll send you a postcard." Before, Grandpa was so focused on Cody's climbing, I could have walked out the door holding a noose and a suicide note and he would have wished me luck. Now he couldn't handle my taking a little trip to Yellowstone, *with a boy.*

I bolted out of my chair when I heard the sound of Marcus's tires crunching pine needles on the driveway. Grandpa gave me a twenty-dollar bill, damp with dishwater. I slung my knapsack over my shoulder. Grandpa followed me out and stood on the porch, glaring at Marcus's car.

Marcus grinned at me when I got in, his teeth porcelain white in the morning sun. He wore frayed denim cutoffs that went down to his knee and a T-shirt with the name of a rock band I didn't recognize. Zachary was sitting in the backseat, a huge picture book draped over his lap, his legs pushed out in front of him, too short to reach the floor. I waved goodbye to Grandpa, who was still standing on the porch with arms folded, the ruffles on his apron stirring in the breeze. "Your granddad is stunning in that apron," Marcus said from the corner of his mouth.

"Flatters his figure," I said. Marcus laughed, which made me feel a little less anxious. I turned around and smiled at Zachary. "It's good to see you again, Zachary. What are you reading?"

He shrugged.

Deep breath. Patience. Patience.

"You lead the way," Marcus said as he backed out of the driveway.

The day was beautiful. The leaves were the new green of early summer, and they looked succulent enough to eat, especially when we reached the part of the park that had been burned in the fire of 1988. The charred skeletons of the older trees were surrounded by thickets of young aspens and pines. Foliage flourished near the blackened roots, and the forest floor was carpeted with wildflowers of every color. Despite the new growth, the blackened trees stood as mementos of that dreadful fiery summer.

I closed my eyes against memories of dreams. Eventually we crossed a little bridge over a creek. I saw a moose grazing in the shallows. "Look, Zachary!" I cried. "A moose!" I glanced back to see that Zachary was still staring into the pages of his book. "Maybe we should buy you a book about Yellowstone, Zachary," I said, "so you don't miss it."

Marcus laughed loudly at that one. "She got you there, Zach!"

Shrug.

At least Marcus thought I was funny.

We took the drive slowly because it seemed like every time we rounded a bend a herd of buffalo was standing in the middle of the road. Each car passing by would slow down to take pictures, and that meant the traffic bunched up like an ice floe. That was okay because the animals were interesting to watch. Besides, I discovered it was kind of fun to be the tour guide. I'm not so good at making conversation, but when you're showing someone around Yellowstone, you always have something to say.

We finally got out of the car at a place called Uncle Tom's Trail, where staircases cling to cliff sides at impossible angles. Marcus and Zachary wanted to take the stairs down into the chasm, and I followed. Holding the railing, I kept my vision fixed ahead, trying not to look down. I made it to the second tier, but from there forward, the stairs were made of metal grating. I could see through my footing to the ground, hundreds of feet below. *So far to fall, so long to know you're going to hit the ground before it happens.* The thought made me dizzy and I couldn't go on.

Marcus looked back at me, seeming to understand. "Want to wait here for us?"

I nodded and sat on a park bench that was nestled against the rock wall. Zachary and Marcus went down the next several hundred steps to look at the waterfall. I could hear it resonating through the canyon. The force of the water seemed to make even the air vibrate, and the sky was filled with mist. I remembered how it had looked to me as a child, a lazy streak of water draping itself over the cliff. With Grandpa's hands closed around my waist, I would stand on the lower rung of the railing and lean into the canyon so I could feel like I was flying over the Yellowstone River. I knew that as long as Grandpa held me, I could never fall.

Nothing scared me then. As a scrawny little kid, I had been as brave as Cody.

Now, every time I glanced toward the bottom of the canyon, I imagined my body, broken and bloody, on the rocks below. Like Gary. Like Cody. I closed my eyes and tried to focus on the birds in their endless refrain, but they seemed to be singing about how beautiful the view was from up there.

Show-offs.

A whole busload of elderly tourists had come and gone before I saw Marcus and Zachary climbing back up the stairs, breathing hard. Zachary's face was full of light. Marcus looked as if he had just witnessed something magical, and he told me about an eagle they had seen through borrowed binoculars swirling and dipping for fish at the base of the falls. I smiled as he told the story, but inside I was jealous. I'd missed it because I was too afraid of a few stairs.

It was already late afternoon before we finally pulled into the parking lot at Old Faithful Inn, one of the largest log buildings in the world. The sloping roof vaults into the sky, and several wings spread in opposite directions like the arms of an octopus. It is probably my favorite building in the whole world, because once you walk inside, you see that the ceiling of the lobby is as high as the roof of a cathedral. Marcus's eyes widened as we entered. Even Zachary seemed impressed. "So we haven't left civilization after all," Marcus said. "What do you say, Zachary?"

The little boy was lost in his own world as he stared into the rafters.

I led them over to the ice cream cart by the French doors that opened out to the geyser area. I have never been to the Old Faithful Inn without getting the delicious ice cream they sell there. I wasn't surprised to learn that Zachary was a plain vanilla kid while Marcus was the chocolate lover. I got my regular pistachio. Without nuts in it, ice cream is just cold air and milk fat.

We looked at the geyser schedule that hung on the log wall. That's why it's called Old Faithful—the geyser's eruptions are so regular they can be predicted to within a few minutes. We had plenty of time to kill until the next eruption, so we strolled up the boardwalks to look at the spring pools dotting the lime-covered hillside behind the inn. The landscape in this area always seems otherworldly to me. The lime makes the soil white, the water is hot enough to scald you, and the ground gives way to incredibly deep caverns filled with water. The walls of each mineral pool are different colors: yellow, blue, green, purple, making the limey hillside look like a giant artist's palette. Even on that hot summer day, columns of steam rose from the pools to mingle with the little white clouds speckling the blue sky.

Zachary wandered ahead of us, licking his ice cream. Marcus looked around at the weird landscape. "I wish I could have come here as a kid. It's beautiful."

I brushed a wisp of hair out of my face. "It's amazing in winter here. There's hardly anyone around. Animals are everywhere. The snowmobiles are loud and smelly, but you can cross-country ski to places where you can't hear them."

Marcus didn't seem to be listening. He was just staring into a pool the color of tangerine sherbet. I was silent for a moment until I thought of something to ask. "Will you and Zachary be spending the school year here?"

"Apparently that's not up to us." His face was taut.

I thought of the pale, haggard woman at the firemen's picnic. "Is your mom doing okay?"

"You ask a lot of questions." He narrowed his eyes at me, then walked up the boardwalk, licking his ice cream cone.

I stood there watching him go, wondering what just

happened. My mouth went dry. I didn't feel like eating ice cream anymore, and I threw it in a trashcan.

Marcus stopped to look into the mineral pool called Heart Spring.

Maybe I shouldn't have brought up his mother. I'd probably embarrassed him. I tentatively walked closer to him and leaned my elbows on the railing near the hot pot. The mineral deposits on the sides of the pool were the blue of a robin's egg. The water inside it was perfectly clear, and deep.

We were quiet until Marcus said, "I didn't mean to snap at you."

"Uh-huh."

"I just have a hard time talking about my parents."

"It's okay."

"I'm really sorry." He turned to look at me. His eyes darted over mine, back and forth, then over the edges of my hair and down my arm, back into the pool. "It's not just my folks. I'm really worried about Zachary." He turned to look up the boardwalk at his brother. Zachary was standing by the little green pool, staring into it, his ice cream melting to cover his hand. "It only happened a month ago, but I really thought that by now he'd be more over it."

"He does seem to be in his own world."

"Mabel has been talking about suing my parents for custody. Dad won't put up much of a fight. He's too busy with that skank he left us for. But Mom would never give up. A court process like that could take years. I don't want that to happen to Zachary. I don't think he could take it."

"That would be hard," I mumbled. I was flattered that he was opening up to me, though I felt a little uncomfortable. I barely knew him. But maybe this was a good sign. I thought he must like me, at least a little, to be talking like this.

"It's just, he doesn't even know Mabel. She's a total

stranger to him. And it's pretty clear Mom can't take care of him, not after what happened." He glanced at me and chuckled grimly. "Your grandpa told you, right? That Mom tried to kill herself?"

I nodded. I had no idea what to say, so I just stood there like an idiot with a sympathetic look on my face, but he didn't seem to mind my silence. He stared into the water and spoke so low it was almost a chant. "Swallowed two packages of sleeping pills while we were at school. Zachary was the one who found her."

"Whoa. *Zachary* found her?"

"Half-conscious, rolling around on the floor in her own puke."

"Jesus." The whole reality of what Zachary was coping with hit me. He wasn't a sullen kid. He didn't hate me. The poor little thing was just shell-shocked, and I'd been too wrapped up in my own problems to see that.

Marcus smiled sadly. "Pretty bad, right?"

"Why did she do it?" I finally asked.

He shrugged. "Because she's an alcoholic? Or because she let my dad slap her around? Because he left her for a sleazeball real estate agent? Because she lost her job? Who knows? Frankly," he added bitterly, "I didn't ask. And now Mabel is suing for custody of Zachary because suddenly she gives a shit."

We stood quietly as a group of tourists swarmed around us, taking pictures and joking cheerfully. Marcus glanced at his watch and mumbled, "It's almost time for Old Faithful." He grinned at me weakly, then looked around. "Where'd Zach go?" I looked toward the green pool. He wasn't there anymore.

I scanned the boardwalks up and down the hill. I couldn't spot him. "Zachary?" I called.

"I hate when he does this," Marcus mumbled.

"He wanders off a lot?"

Marcus walked quickly up the hill, yelling, "Zach!

Zach! Come on! We have to go soon if we want to see Old Faithful!"

I walked behind him, edging around some tourists staring into a pool. One of the older men muttered, "What a way to go." He was pointing at the bones of a moose, white and stark, deep in the hot water. It had been boiled to death.

We had to find Zachary *now*.

Up the boardwalk I heard a frantic burst of noise. A park ranger was standing near the top of the hill, blowing a whistle like crazy and waving his arms. Marcus broke into a run. I struggled to keep up with him, fighting off the image of Zachary scalded like that poor moose. We wove through tourists at a full gallop, but it didn't feel fast enough. The ranger turned and yelled to another ranger, "Dave! Find the parents!" I was close enough to see he was red-faced as he peered into the basin of a mineral pool, but I couldn't see what he was looking at.

Finally, when we got level with him, I saw Zachary. He was standing on the lip of the hot pool, the toes of his sneakers nearly touching the boiling water. His hands were in his pockets and he was staring absently at the ranger.

I hated myself in that instant. I should have told him how thin the crust was around the pools. He might be standing on nothing more than a quarter inch of brittle limestone. I was so terrified I started shaking.

"Zachary!" Marcus yelled. "What are you doing?"

The ranger looked at Marcus. "Is he with you?" The man was furious.

"I turned my back for just a second!"

The ranger ignored him and spoke to Zachary. "Now, son, I want you to back up real slow like, okay? Only walk where you walked before. Can you do that for me?"

Zachary turned around and looked at Marcus with the same absent stare he'd turned on me so many times. "Do it, Zach. Like he says," Marcus pleaded.

Zachary's brows furrowed. He didn't seem to understand what the big deal was.

Impatiently, the ranger said, "I'm not kidding, son. You're in a bit of danger there."

Zachary looked at Marcus once more, then slowly backed away from the lip of the pool until he touched the boardwalk. Marcus knelt down and pulled him up, hugging him close. He kept saying, "Jesus, Zachary. Jesus."

The ranger waited until Marcus stood back up, then pointed his finger in his face. "Get him the hell out of this area," he said, then turned on his heel and marched away.

We walked very slowly down the boardwalk, too shaken to talk. At the bottom, we sat on one of the benches that were arranged in a crescent around a cone of lime—the mouth of Old Faithful. I had to sit on my hands to keep them from trembling. Marcus kept his hand on Zachary's shoulder the whole time.

"You gotta stay near us, okay, Zach?" Marcus said, his voice unsteady.

The little boy nodded, panting a little. What happened had been upsetting, but in a strange way, the jolt seemed to have done him good. His cheeks were flushed and he seemed more awake than I'd ever seen him.

There was already a large crowd milling around, calling to each other noisily. Two little blond boys about Zachary's age were running back and forth on the boardwalk, ignoring the stern warning signs everywhere that said not to run. I looked at Zachary, who was sitting slumped, staring into space, already receding into himself again. It was amazing how subdued he was compared to other kids his age. I wished I had been gentler with him. Poor little guy.

A great surging noise burst through the turmoil of the crowd, and all voices were silenced. The little blond boys ran to their parents.

Steam and hot water rose to the rim of the geyser, sounding like breaking waves at high tide. The board-walk under our feet started to shake. Zachary grabbed hold of Marcus's thick forearm.

Suddenly the geyser sent a column of hot water roaring into the sky like a furious serpent. The spray was cooled by the breeze as it drifted our way, wetting our faces. We squinted against the fury. I could feel the vibration of thousands of gallons of water shooting into the air with more force than a million cannons. The water rose in an angry column for more time than seemed possible. I felt tiny.

Then the column wilted and lashed around, weakening. It gushed out a couple more times, then finally subsided under the huge white cloud it had sent into the sky.

The crowd erupted into applause.

Zachary was still staring at the cone of lime. Marcus pulled up his T-shirt and wiped the water off his face, beaming.

"What did you think, guys?" I asked.

Marcus shook his head, stupefied. "That was awesome."

I laughed and turned to Zachary. "Not bad for a natural phenomenon, huh?"

The little boy was speechless, as usual, but he was smiling. I'd never seen him do that. He was a beautiful kid when he smiled.

13

The next day, as he tugged his satchel into the house, Zachary forced himself to smile in my direction, which I could see cost him a great deal of effort. But when I cheerily listed a dozen things for us to do, he went back to shrugging, and I got no further response. I flopped down on Grandpa's sunken sofa, defeated. "Well, believe me, Zachary, this wasn't my idea."

"Mine neither." His voice came out in a throaty whisper.

I realized this was the first time he'd said anything to me at all. Was this progress? I tried to think of a way I could keep him talking. "Yellowstone was fun, huh?"

Shrug.

I tried another tack. "Marcus sure thinks you're a cool kid."

Shrug.

I sat there, studying him, going over all the things I'd tried with him. I hadn't gotten anywhere with doing activities, ignoring him or joking with him. Maybe the brutally honest approach would work. "You know, Zachary, we'll have more fun if you just talk to me. Because right now, this is awful for both of us."

He looked at me, surprised, then dropped the satchel onto the floor and sat down on it with his chin in his hands. I thought I'd really messed up this time, that he would tell Marcus I'd been mean and that would be the end of everything, but finally, through pink, wet lips, he mumbled, "I miss Mommy."

Success! I tried to keep the triumph out of my voice. "I'm sure you do."

"Can we call her?" Every part of him seemed to get taller with the question.

I hadn't expected this. "I don't know the number, Zachary," I fumbled.

He reached into his satchel and pulled out a slip of paper. "I do."

I paused, not sure what I should do. Zachary was finally talking to me, and I just didn't feel right about denying him. But it seemed risky, considering what Marcus had told me about a custody battle between Mabel and Penny. I had a feeling Mabel wouldn't like it. And after the furious way he'd talked about his mom, I was sure Marcus wouldn't. But how could I tell a little boy he couldn't talk to his own mother?

I was still looking at Zachary with my mouth open, not sure what to say, when he shrugged, picked up the phone himself and dialed.

Too late now.

He straightened up at attention as he said, "Hello, can I talk to my mom?—Penelope Stanislov. Can I please talk to her?—Can you get her?—Can she call me later?—The phone number is . . ." He drew a blank and looked at me, helpless. I sighed, took the phone from him and gave the man on the other end Grandpa's number. As I hung up, Zachary looked devastated, but his view of me seemed to have changed completely. Now he looked me in the eye and said, "Thanks, Annie."

"Anytime, Zachary." I'd barely said it when the phone rang. Zachary jumped to pick it up.

"Hello?" he practically yelled. "Mommy? Mommy! I miss you!" He plopped on the sofa, his feet dangling over the edge of the cushions. His whole body seemed to relax into enormous relief. "I'm at Annie's house. She's taking care of me. What are you doing? Are they nice to you? Are you getting better?"

I felt like I was eavesdropping, so I moved into the kitchen and started getting lunch ready so he could talk to his mom in private. Every so often I would sneak a look at him. His face changed by the minute, from joy, to grief, to worry, and back to joy. Everything that had happened must have been so confusing for him. I could see, though, that talking to his mom did him good.

I was cutting up carrot sticks when Zachary said, "Annie, Mom wants to talk to you."

I froze. I really didn't want to talk to her. I didn't want to get any more involved than I already was. But Zachary was holding the phone out for me, and I couldn't very well refuse it. "Hello?"

"Hello, Annie?" Her voice was hoarse.

"Yes. Hi."

"I just wanted to say thanks for letting Zachary call me."

"Sure."

"I'm not supposed to talk on the phone more than a few times a week, but the day nurse here makes exceptions for young children."

"That's . . . nice."

"The night staff are more strict. So I'm hoping it's okay if I call Zachary at your house? When he's there? Would that be okay?"

She sounded as though she'd been spread over concrete, and I couldn't say no. "Sure. He'll be here most weekdays until six."

"Thanks, Annie." She sighed. "You don't know—"

"Anytime."

After we hung up, I sat next to Zachary on the couch, trying to hide how much talking to his mom had stressed me out. I'd have to deal with that later. "Your mom's going to call you here, Zachary. Won't that be nice?"

He nodded. His whole body was melted like caramel, and his eyes were still and pulled down at the corners. Talking to her must have reminded him of how far away she really was. He carefully folded the paper that had his mom's phone number written on it and tucked it into the satchel, seeming to have a place just for that purpose.

I'd never seen him without that satchel. "What do you have in there, Zach?"

"Books," he muttered.

"Cool. I love books. Can I see?"

Reluctantly, he shuffled over, dragging the heavy satchel behind him. He plopped onto the sofa next to me, unstrapped the bag and pulled out the most beautiful edition of J.R.R. Tolkien's *Lord of the Rings* I had ever seen. The silvery blue cover was brightly illustrated with all the best characters from Middle Earth. Gandalf the wizard stood in the center with his long arms outstretched, and beside him were Frodo and Bilbo Baggins, the hobbits; Elrond and all his elves; the dwarves; and Gollum. The Dark Lord Sauron hovered over them all, only his sinister eyes visible from underneath a cloak.

"What a beautiful book," I whispered. He nodded proudly, then reached back into his satchel to pull out more books, all my favorites: the Chronicles of Narnia, *The Phantom Tollbooth, A Wrinkle in Time.* "Zachary, do you read these by yourself?"

He shrugged.

I remembered the direct approach had worked before, so I said, "Did you know it's rude to shrug when someone asks you a question?" He looked up at me, surprised. "You can read these by yourself?" I asked again.

He nodded. "I'm a good reader."

"That's amazing, Zachary!"

He shrugged, caught himself and said, "Marcus taught me when I was little."

"Still, you must be a pretty smart person." He seemed proud of the compliment. Was I finally reaching him? "Would you like to just sit around and read today?"

His little chest deflated with relief. "Okay."

I realized I felt relieved, too.

Zachary, dwarfed behind the huge Tolkien book, sat with his ratty sneakers propped up on Grandpa's coffee table. I cuddled myself into the old, beat-up easy chair draped with Grandma's denim quilt, cradling *Wuthering Heights* in my lap. We didn't move for hours.

There is something about just reading with someone. It lays your doubts to rest, for a while at least, and you can relax into your book and not think of things to say. For most people, silence is the hardest thing of all to endure. But with certain people, like Zachary, it's easy to keep silent. It united us—saying nothing, letting the whisper of the wind against the cabin walls do all the talking for us.

When Marcus came to pick him up, Zachary looked disappointed and smiled at me apologetically. I tousled his hair as he walked toward the car. There were gray circles under Marcus's eyes, but he still brightened when he saw me.

"Hi, Annie. Thought you might like to take a walk or something."

"That would be lovely." *Lovely?* Did I really say that? I was obviously spending so much time reading, I was starting to sound like Emily Brontë. As I got in the car next to Marcus, I made a mental note not to talk like a Victorian-era nerd.

After we dropped Zachary off at Mabel's, I directed Marcus down the park road to a place called Kelly Warm Springs, a natural pool that is so hot, snow melts as it falls on the banks, and the grass stays green all year round. We strolled around the pond, listening to the chatter of the frogs and crickets.

I was glad Marcus wasn't talkative because I didn't know if I could carry a conversation. I felt guilty. I didn't know if I should tell him about his mom and Zachary talking. I was afraid if he found out, he would think I was betraying him. What if Zachary told him, though?

Marcus yawned like a tiger.

"You look tired," I said, opting for the wait-and-see plan.

He rubbed his back and winced. "We had a rough day of cutting," he said, then suddenly looked at me in surprise, as if he'd let a secret slip.

"Cutting?" I asked. He was acting funny, and it made me curious. "Do you work for a lumber company or something?"

He shrugged, just like Zachary. "It's not . . . I'm just . . ." He looked around as though he'd been trapped.

"You're not doing anything . . . illegal, are you?" I'd heard of people growing marijuana in the forests.

He rolled his eyes. "I work at the lumberyard in town, okay?"

"Oh. Okay."

"I'm not exactly advertising it. And I'd appreciate it if you didn't tell anyone. At all. Especially not your grandpa or Mabel."

"Why not?" He wasn't making any sense.

"Because it's my personal business, okay?"

"Fine." I took a couple of steps backward. He was acting so weird I suddenly felt a little wary of him. Why keep his job a secret? "I don't get it, but whatever."

"I'm just working to save up some money, and I don't want Mabel to know about it. Blame it on my trust issues if you want, but please don't tell anyone, okay?"

It was very weird, but I could sympathize with trust issues. "I won't tell anyone, Marcus. I barely talk to anyone anyway."

"That's true. You are kind of quiet." He smiled, but looked worried again. "You think I'm a total jerk?"

"Not *totally*," I joked, but the truth was, I wasn't sure what I thought. He seemed a little volatile, but maybe I liked how unpredictable he was. I studied him. He was nervously biting his bottom lip, and there was something strange about the jittery way he kept glancing at me. I guessed he was holding something back, but he obviously didn't want to talk any more about it.

He bent to pick up a few rocks and tried to skip one across the water. It plunked to the bottom of the pond. He casually flung another rock, pretending he had never meant to skip that other one in the first place. I couldn't help giggling at him. He turned around and said, "What?" But a grin began at the corner of his mouth.

I smiled and picked out a stone. "Rest the flat side on your middle finger." I showed him how I was holding it, then threw my stone across. It skipped four times.

Marcus raised his eyebrows, impressed. "Good arm."

"You try."

He lined up his arm perfectly, pulled back with flawless form, and threw the stone at the precise angle I had shown him. It smacked the surface of the water and sank right to the bottom. "Damn."

"I forgot to mention," I said, half joking, "only the pure of heart can do it."

"Ha ha." He grinned at me, then dropped his gaze. "I'm sorry I keep snapping at you."

"Yeah," I said. "You can be pretty touchy."

"I don't mean to, Annie. I like you. It's just that I've

got so much going on." He squinted at the horizon, which was already starting to darken. "I guess that's no excuse."

It was true; he'd been through a lot. Besides, I wasn't exactly in a position to point fingers for being moody. "I don't need excuses. An apology is enough."

He shook his head as if to clear it, then picked up another stone and flung it at the water. This time, it skipped twice. "Cool," he said.

"See? Only the pure of heart."

"Yeah, yeah." He smiled at me again, then bent to pick out another stone.

We stayed there until it was nearly dark, skipping rocks and talking, then he drove me home. I was standing on the porch watching him back out of the driveway when I realized it had been almost three hours since I'd thought about Cody.

With a deep pang, I wished I could talk with him, just for a few minutes, about anything. Even climbing.

14

"Why do you love to climb so much?"

We're sitting in the Tepee Tree, invisible to the world beneath the blue-green branches that droop to the ground like a sticky ball gown. I'm flattered that you're sharing your secret place with me. You're leaning back on your elbows, your long legs stuck out in front of you, your arctic eyes running over the branches that surround us. "I don't know, Annie. I guess climbing is like going to church for me."

I laugh. Unless there's a bake sale going on inside, neither of us has set foot in a church since Grandma's funeral ten years ago. "How would you know what it's like to be in a church?"

"It's hard to explain." You are squeezing the rubber ball while you think about it. You're always squeezing that damn thing. As good as you are, you always want to be better, stronger. I know that your determination is what makes you such an amazing climber, but sometimes I wish that hanging out with me was enough for once.

"One of these days I'm going to hide that ball from you."

"Shut up."

"Some guys your age have learned to squeeze other things."

"Shut up."

"Why won't you just put it down for a second? God!"

"Shut up, Miss Bitchy Boss."

"Seriously," I say, trying to shift to the grown-up-sounding tone you seem to appreciate. "What's so great about climbing?" I lean my chin in my hand to show I'm giving you my rapt attention.

"I don't know if I can explain it." You lie on your back and stare into the branches above. For a second you stop squeezing the ball, and your eyes seem to lose focus. "When you're holding on to a rock wall, you have to trust it. Your life depends on your grip, your foothold, whatever anchor you have your rope on. But mostly, I guess, you have to trust yourself, because fear makes you freeze up. Sometimes you have no idea what your next move will be, but you have to know you can do it anyway. You can't think about anything else. That kind of concentration is sort of like . . . a devotion. You know?"

"No, I don't."

"Yes you do. You get that same feeling when you're staring through your camera. I've seen you." You lean up on your elbow, impatient with me. "The other day, when you snapped that beaver dragging that huge tree? I'd never seen anyone look so happy in my life. And every day since you sent off that film, you've run to the mailbox looking for the slides, even though you know they won't be here for at least another week."

"So I have a hobby. Big deal. I'm not like you."

"Yeah, I'm a climber. A good one, sure, but not like back in the day when Grandpa was opening up routes on every major peak in the Rockies." You give me a sideways fluttering look. "You have a gift." You say this haltingly, as if it's something you hate admitting.

And that's why I almost believe you.

15

The cottonwood trees were in full bloom. Small white tufts of delicate fuzz drifted through the cool air like snow. Zachary, panting, looked at the blizzard curiously, so I stopped and caught one of the puffs between my palms. "These are cottonwood seeds, Zachary." Gingerly, I handed it to him before the breeze could take it away. Pointing to one of the stately trees surrounding us, I said, "A huge tree like that one grows fifty feet high and lives for a hundred years from just one of these little puffs. If you look carefully, in the middle of the cotton you'll see a tiny black dot. That's the seed."

He fingered the white fluff and smiled a little as he looked at the fleecy cotton swirling around him. "It makes the forest seem like magic."

"All forests are magic," I whispered. He seemed to take me very seriously as he peered through the leaves around us.

He was much cheerier than earlier that morning. As soon as Mabel dropped him off, his mom called, but she could only talk for a minute before her group therapy. After he hung up, Zachary sank into the sofa and stared at the floor. I took in his droopy eyes and pale limbs—bookworm trademarks—and decided he needed exercise. I made him empty his satchel of all but one book, packed a lunch for us, and we headed down one of the trails that snaked off behind Grandpa's cabin. He hadn't liked the idea, but he was stronger than he looked, and he hardly complained at all as he trudged behind me into the woods.

We were in the old, dense part of the forest. Sunlight filtered through the leaves to land at our feet in thin wisps. The breeze was just enough to keep the cotton dancing in the air, glowing like daylight fireflies. Clingy moss made the trees look like stooped-over old men, which must be why they call it grandfather moss. It did look like an enchanted forest. I grinned at Zachary. "Kind of makes you feel like Bilbo Baggins, doesn't it?"

Zachary perked up. Wearing his satchel like a backpack, and with his big feet and thick dark hair, he could have passed for a hobbit. Next to his small frame I felt as tall as an elf. We stood taking in the gentle air for a while, then went on at a brisk pace.

The trail forked several times, and each time I took the left fork so we wouldn't get lost. We walked for a couple of hours until we came to a clearing where hundreds of red, purple, and yellow wildflowers drank in the sun. Young aspen saplings shimmered and shook their silver leaves.

I stopped short. I hadn't meant to come here. The Tepee Tree stood right next to us, near where the trail opened into the field. The tips of its huge bottom branches skirted the ground, swaying with the breeze. I looked at it as if it had appeared from nowhere, the result of some sinister magic. I'd just been thinking about this place!

When Cody brought me here once, he took a

circuitous route so I wouldn't be able to find it on my own. He came here to hide from the world, and he didn't want me to know exactly where it was. Seeing it for the first time since losing him sucked me downward. I couldn't breathe.

"Annie?" Zachary was looking at me quizzically.

Deep breath. Don't fall apart. Come back to the now. Those days are gone, passed down a long river of days.

But the tree was still here.

I squinted hard at Zachary, forcing a smile. "Did I space out there?"

He nodded.

"I've been known to do that."

"Me too." He smiled crookedly at me. It seemed like he understood. Maybe grief leaves a trace on a person, like a hint of smoke only certain people can smell, certain people whose worlds have burned down, too. Darla. Marcus. Zachary.

I looked at his face. He already seemed like a different boy. His cheeks were flushed from exertion, and the blue half-moons under his eyes no longer looked like bruises. He turned from me to peer with curiosity through the green needles of the tree.

It felt like pulling open a wound, but I parted the branches and walked in with Zachary behind me. We were in a large tepee made of deep green velvet. The fragrant pine branches hung around us in a circle, and the thick trunk stood like a pillar. I pictured Cody, leaning back on an elbow, squeezing that damn rubber ball. A part of him still lingered, and I wanted to spend some time with it even though it hurt to be here. "This is a good place for lunch, wouldn't you say, Zachary?"

He was already unzipping his satchel, pulling out his book.

I spread out the tarp as Zachary bunched up his bag to make a pillow for his head. The light filtering through the branches was soft and green, and I felt protected, lying where Cody had lain, eating cheese and crackers and slices of apple. Zachary lost himself in his book. After a while I laid my head on the rough cushion of fallen pine needles and fell asleep. I was so exhausted from nights of fitful sleep, I was out for hours.

The sound of evening crickets drew me out of my doze. I looked at my wrist and discovered I had forgotten to put on my watch. "What time did Mabel say she was coming for you, Zachary?"

"Six." He was sitting up, rubbing his eyes.

"We'd better get a move on." Meeting Mabel wasn't the only reason to hurry. Marcus and I had made plans to go out for dinner, and I had wanted to get home early enough to take a shower and change clothes. Not that this was a date exactly. Most of the time it felt like we were just friends, but every so often he would give me a look that made my heart race. Still, even if it wasn't a date, I sure didn't want to show up wearing a sweaty Girl Scout T-shirt.

We rolled up the tarp with all our trash inside and stuffed it into my backpack. When we stepped through the tree branches and I saw the long shadows on the ground, my heart sank. It was already late afternoon. We would definitely be late. I turned to Zachary apologetically. "Are you up to jogging a ways?" He nodded, but didn't seem very sure.

I broke into a slow trot. I was proud of Zachary, the way he kept putting one foot in front of the other like a little trooper. I thought we might even make it on time.

When you're wandering in the woods, nothing looks the same coming as it does going. Changes in light at different times of day can make trees look different and the trail harder to follow. It's easy to second-guess yourself if you don't know exactly where you are. But it was okay because I did know exactly where we were.

Until we came to a three-pronged fork in the trail.

I stopped abruptly.

I didn't exactly remember a three-pronged fork in the trail. I had taken every left turn so we could take every right turn to get back home. The method doesn't work too well when you have two right turns in front of you.

Zachary stomped behind me impatiently. "What's wrong?" His voice sounded tired and anxious.

"We turn right here," I said, hoping he didn't notice the doubt in my voice.

With Zachary's short, unsure stride behind me, I headed down the right-most fork. Now, instead of kindly grandfathers, the trees were creepy old men. I fought down the panicky feeling that I might have gotten poor Zachary lost.

After a few minutes our surroundings began to look familiar and I realized that we were on the same trail Grandpa and I had taken to Darla's cabin. I calmed down—we could use Darla's phone to call Mabel and tell her where we were.

The pines gave way to aspens as we entered Darla's grove. I sighed with relief when I saw Grandpa's truck parked outside.

"Zachary, we might not be late after all!" I said. "My grandpa's here and he can give us a ride!"

"Oh, good!" he said, and dropped his satchel on the ground.

Maybe if I hadn't been huffing and puffing when I approached the front door, I would have heard the sounds coming from inside the cabin right away. But I'd raised my hand to knock before I heard the unmistakable squeak of bedsprings—the *rhythmic* squeak of bedsprings.

And grunting.

And moaning.

I froze. My cheeks heated. This couldn't be. *Grandpa? And Darla?* I had thought Grandpa acted a little weird around her, but *this*? *This* never entered my mind! It didn't even seem possible. It was too *gross* to be possible!

I glanced over at Zachary, who looked at me in confusion as he listened. I shifted my weight, and the floorboards under me issued a long, shrill whine.

I froze again.

Don't make a sound. They can't know I'm here. Don't. Move.

I stood so still I could feel sweat seeping from the pores on my upper lip.

I heard Darla murmur, "Oh, Jack!" My grandfather made a caveman sound. Their rhythm changed.

They seemed to be reaching some kind of . . . conclusion.

Every neuron in my body demanded that I *leave now*. But quietly. Very, very quietly.

I turned from Darla's front door and toward the steps. I was stealthy, completely silent, every muscle fluid like the rippling physique of a mountain lion as I backed away.

Right into a huge metal garbage can.

Pop bottles rolled, aluminum cans crunched, old mustard jars shattered, brown newspaper crinkled, and the garbage can lid spun on the porch boards like a coin. I was lying on a mound of soggy tea bags and banana peels.

I heard bare feet hit the floor inside. Grandpa was shouting something about a gun, and Darla squealed about unnecessary violence.

Oh God, he's coming out.

I tried to get up to run but I kept slipping on the slime underneath me. "Zachary!" I pleaded. "Help me!" But he just stood there holding his belly, red-faced and laughing.

Grandpa lunged through the front door with a

rolling pin spinning in his hand. He was wearing a paper towel. And nothing else.

When he saw me lying there, he turned gray. Then he turned white. Then he turned tomato red. He just stood there staring at me, as if unaware that he was completely naked.

I was painfully aware of it.

He flexed his jaw several times before he found his voice. "Hello, Annie."

I moved one hand from underneath a cantaloupe rind and waved.

Then he saw Zachary out of the corner of his eye. He nodded formally. "Hi, son."

Zachary nodded and doubled over laughing.

As he began his retreat, Grandpa dropped the rolling pin and stretched the paper towel, trying to cover more of himself.

It ripped clean down the middle.

I winced and shielded my eyes. I heard Grandpa scurry back into the cabin.

From inside I heard Darla start to giggle, then laugh out loud, and finally give in to uncontrollable howls. Wheezing with effort, she calmed herself down and stepped out the door. At least she had a robe on. "Anna, I'm so sorry," she managed to say, but when she saw me lying in a pile of garbage, she lost all control.

I grabbed the porch railing and pulled myself out of the mess, saying, "We were, uh, lost."

"Oh dear, Anna." Darla wiped her eyes, making a herculean effort to stop laughing. "What a surprise you've had!"

I had no idea what to say, so I shrugged.

"I'd better tend to Jack, dear. Wait just a minute, will you?" She went back inside, calling, "Jack? Come out, darling!"

I sat on the top step, holding myself. Grandpa and

Darla? Having sex? What did Darla see in him? She was so nice and bubbly and interesting. Grandpa was stern and boring. I didn't get it. A picture I'd rather not describe flashed in my mind. I shuddered as though I'd just taken a long swig of curdled milk. *They're so old!*

I looked over at Zachary. "You won't tell Marcus about this, will you?"

The little worm nodded. "He's going to love this."

"Zachary, please, you can't tell Marcus." I tried to look very serious.

He looked at me with an evil little grin. "This is the best thing since Grandma's girdle came undone in the movie theater!"

I let my head fall to my knees. As if things between Grandpa and me weren't already uncomfortable! Thank God I had an excuse to be out later that night, but I couldn't avoid him forever. What would I say? What would *he* say?

Darla reappeared on the porch, this time wearing blue jeans and a Pink Floyd T-shirt. She smiled sheepishly and whispered so Zachary couldn't hear. "Well, Anna, I assume you've gathered that your grandfather and I are romantically involved." I nodded, unable to meet her eyes, and she patted my shoulder. "I hope it wasn't too much for you to see your grandfather stripped . . . of his dignity, so to speak?"

I shook my head. I was so full of weird emotions, I couldn't really talk. I didn't know if I felt embarrassed or mad or angry or hurt. I had a strange, weepy feeling but it made no sense to me. Why should I care if Grandpa had a girlfriend? I shook my head and tried to apologize. "I'm sorry—"

Darla waved away my words. "My dear, there is no need to apologize. I'm the one at fault. Your grandfather has been after me to get a bear-proof Dumpster," she said, a twinkle in her eye.

I laughed uncomfortably.

She pulled my grandfather's truck keys out of her hip pocket and handed them to me. "Can you manage to get yourselves back home?"

I didn't have a driver's license, but I knew how to drive. Cody often let me take the wheel on the dirt roads that snaked between the cabins. Besides, I would have stolen a car to get out of there.

I thanked Darla, got Zachary into the truck, and sped away.

16

"So!" Marcus said when he picked me up for dinner. "I hear Grandpa's doing the horizontal tango with some English chick!"

"Oh God." I let my hair drape over my face as I buckled my seat belt. "Is that what Zachary said?"

"His version involved the term *pee-pee*." He shot me a devilish grin as he backed out of the driveway. "I inferred the rest."

"Can we just not talk about it?"

"What?" he asked innocently. "You don't enjoy picturing your grandpa *having sex*?"

"Marcus."

"*Doing* it?"

"Shut up."

"Senior scrogging?"

"Stop!"

"His wrinkly lips on her wrinkly—"

"That's it! I'll never think about sex again."

"Hold your horses, Mother Teresa."

"Turn right here."

Dornan's Restaurant sits atop a ridge of sagebrush

that overlooks the easy meandering of the Snake River. Marcus and I sat outside at the grill. Our hamburgers came with dollops of yellow potato salad and Cokes in real glasses with thick wedges of lemon. We ate, slapping intermittently at mosquitoes, watching the amber light turn to purple as the sun settled behind the mountains. The Tetons stood over us, jagged and violet, their tops cut off by a thick canopy of clouds. A storm was threatening to bubble over the horizon. "It's beautiful here," Marcus said, his eyes on mine.

I took in a breath. I'd read about romantic moments like this in books, never really thinking it might happen to me. But it was happening. Here was a gorgeous guy looking at me with what can only be described as ardor, and I didn't want to waste the moment. I took a deep breath to gather my courage and looked right into his dark, shadowed eyes. "I'm glad I met you," I said, and smiled shyly. For an armadillo type, saying something like this was a big step.

Again his eyes passed over my face, then trailed down the braid that snaked over my shoulder. "Annie, you're so great."

"Thanks. No I'm not."

"But I don't want you to get the wrong idea."

My face went cold. I pulled my hands off the table and folded them in my lap. "What do you mean?"

He shook his head. "It's just, I don't know what the future is going to be."

"Well, neither do I."

"I don't want to lead you on."

"You're not," I said as casually as I could, but I couldn't look at him. I felt totally humiliated and rejected, even if I shouldn't have. We'd just met, after all. It wasn't like he was my boyfriend. I stared hard at the mountains, picked up my hamburger, and took a bite to show how little I cared about what he was saying. It tasted like moss.

"Annie, I really like you."

I nodded, dropping my gaze to the river.

"I do. Seriously. You're really cute and . . . I don't know."

"It's no problem." I shook my head and tried to laugh, knowing how fake it looked. "I meant, I'm glad we're *friends*."

He studied me worriedly. "I am too." He seemed unsure about what to say next.

I methodically chewed my food, staring at the sunset. Marcus squinted across the water. A far-off rattle of a woodpecker sounded, then faded with the light of the evening.

"Can I trust you with something?" he finally asked.

I looked at him. He was biting his bottom lip—the same hesitant expression he'd had at Kelly Warm Springs when I suspected he was hiding something. "What is it?"

"I need complete secrecy." His voice was firm, his eyes solid steel. He was so intense. Whatever this was, it was big.

"Like I said before," I answered, "I hardly talk to anyone."

"I'm serious."

"I won't tell anyone."

He clenched his fists and sat in silence for a minute. There was something volcanic under his surface, and he seemed to be pressing down on it. "All right," he groaned, as if his voice were a valve releasing steam. "If I tell you this, you'll understand everything, but—"

"Marcus," I said, my voice low. "You can trust me."

He took a deep breath. Looking at the mountains behind me, he seemed to be surveying the landscape of what he was about to say. "Zachary and I are going to take off soon."

"Is your mom getting better?" I asked, not understanding why that would be a secret.

"She'll never get better." He licked his lips as he

regarded me. "I'm taking Zachary away." He stared in my eyes until I understood his meaning.

"Wait. You mean—"

"I'm not going to stand by and let Mabel and Mom tear him apart. He needs stability." His words sounded rehearsed, as if he'd planned out his argument like one of those trial lawyers on TV. "I'm going to take him away and raise him myself."

I felt my mouth hanging open. I probably looked like a fool, but I was so shocked I didn't care.

"I'm working, to save money to get us set up. That's why Mabel can't know about my job."

"Marcus—"

"I've been the only reliable person in his life. I've practically raised him myself. I know what's involved. I can do it." He paused, seeming to check the effect his words were having on me.

"Couldn't you go to jail?" My voice sailed to a pitch that matched the enormity of what he was saying. What about Mabel? What about Penny, that thin, desperate woman who called Zachary every day he was with me? "Marcus, are you sure this is a good idea?"

"Mabel and Mom could be fighting over him for years. I can take him somewhere safe and raise him away from that."

"Yeah, but—"

He interrupted me. "I thought you would see it my way." He reached for my hand, wrapping his callused fingers around mine. He was smooth, too smooth, too casual about the way he was touching me, and yet I couldn't ignore what it was doing to me. "I wanted to tell you," he said, "but I was scared you might blow my secret."

"I think you should think about what you're saying." I reluctantly settled my fingers between his, even though everything about this unsettled me. "I mean, you don't really want to raise a child!"

"Yes, I do. I've thought about it a lot."

"What about Mabel?"

"She's not that attached." He gave me a crooked smile and moved his thumb over the veins on my wrist, pressing lightly. "You have soft skin."

"Maybe you should wait to see what happens." He shook his head. "Marcus, you can't just leave."

"Yes I can."

"No you can't."

"In two months I'll be eighteen."

"So?"

"So, I'll be an adult." His voice dropped to a firm place. "I can take care of him, Annie. I have so far."

"I know. I'm not talking about that. I'm talking about . . . people."

"You're talking about people who've done nothing but screw up our lives. From the time we were babies." His sights fixed on the darkening horizon. The air smelled like rain. "We're better off this way. Believe me."

I looked out over the Snake River as it headed downhill to another valley.

"You know, I'm really glad you're here," he said, his voice taking on an intimate tone. "I thought this summer would be nothing but fighting with Mabel and working like a mule." He tried to look meaningfully at me. "I'm glad I met you, Annie."

"I am too, Marcus, but—"

"You're so pretty, do you know that?"

"I'm not." I was confused. I was trying to get my footing in the conversation, but he kept pulling the rug out from under me, right toward him.

A distant crackle of thunder circled its way around the valley. The gray of dusk was turning quickly to charcoal.

Marcus studied me nervously. "I shouldn't have told you," he finally said.

"I'm just confused."

"You're not going to tell anyone, are you?"

"You don't know Mabel like I do." I hated the thought of Mabel getting hurt like this. Everything about her took up a lot of space, but she was a good person. When I was little, I stayed with her when Cody and Grandpa went on overnight climbs. She showed me how to roll up leftover piecrust to make cinnamon pinwheels, and she never made a fuss if I dropped one of them on the floor. Marcus couldn't know the great things about her if she'd never been a part of his life. "She wants to help you and Zachary."

"She never came to see us. She hardly ever called!" The air around us seemed to tremble with his voice. "And now suddenly she's the answer to our problems?"

He leaned his forehead on the palm of his hand. Under any other circumstances I would never have dreamed of touching him, but now it seemed the most natural thing in the world to reach out my hand and rest it on his arm. He was breathing hard, but he leaned into my touch. "It's going to be all right," I said.

"Don't tell anyone, okay?" He took hold of my wrist and moved my hand until it cupped his cheek. I could feel the hard angle of his jaw under my palm and the lift of his throat as he spoke. "Please, Annie, just give me some time. Promise you won't say anything."

"I won't tell anyone." I didn't decide this until after I said it. I knew I was taking a risk, but he hadn't left yet. I thought Mabel might have time to get through to him. Besides, there was something a little dramatic about the way he was telling me all this, as if he were putting on a show. It just didn't seem real. I knew, though, there was only one way I could guarantee secrecy. "I won't tell anyone if you promise to let me know before you go," I said firmly as the first drops of rain fell around us. "You won't just disappear."

He looked at me with serious eyes. "I'll let you know."

17

The cabin was dark when Marcus dropped me off. I stood on the porch, staring at the doorknob.

I couldn't face Grandpa tonight, not after his X-rated debut that afternoon.

If I was really quiet, maybe he wouldn't wake up.

I took off my shoes and left them on the porch, opened the front door in silent increments, and eased it back into its casing so slowly the ancient hinge forgot to complain. In my stocking feet I tiptoed along the only floorboard I knew didn't creak, decided I could do without brushing my teeth, and started up the loft ladder.

I would have made it if I hadn't forgotten to skip the third rung. It squealed on me, and Grandpa called softly from his bedroom, "Annie, is that you?"

I froze halfway up the ladder. "No," I answered.

I heard him get out of bed and come to the doorway. I didn't want any light, but he turned on the lamp on his dresser. His face looked drawn and tired, his pajamas rumpled, his hair flat on one side and puffy on the other. "Where you been?"

"I was with Marcus."

"It's late."

"I know." I flicked my eyes at his midriff, afraid if I raised them any farther he would think it was an invitation to talk.

Once again, the armadillo defense failed me. He coughed once, then forced out, "I'm sorry about this afternoon."

I couldn't say anything. I didn't want to deal with this in any kind of direct way. The whole thing was too icky for me to even think about. I shrugged.

"It's a while since a woman's—"

"Grandpa, please." I hung closer to the ladder, rested my forehead on the back of my hand.

He sighed. "Darla, well, she's—" He swallowed hard. "I care about her."

"That's good."

"Maybe someday you'll understand what that means."

"I know what it means," I snapped. He could be so condescending sometimes.

"No, I mean . . ." His voice sputtered out; he took a deep breath. "What it means to lose someone—When your grandmother—"

"I understand about losing someone, Grandpa." My voice was hard.

"I mean, what it is to lose a lover." He sounded small. I looked at him. He was staring off to the side, watching a memory. With the dim light behind him, his eyes took on a warm navy hue. For the first time I saw a hint of the man who'd written that beautiful letter, begging his wife to come back to him.

But I couldn't understand how he could be interested in anyone. Cody was dead, and he was having affairs with English anthropologists.

"Darla likes you," he said with a grin.

I shrugged.

He nodded sheepishly and turned to go back into his room, but stopped and looked at me. "Marcus. He's good to you?"

"Yes, Grandpa." He made it sound so formal and proper.

He studied me as if to verify that I'd spoken the truth. For a moment I was afraid that the secret I was hiding about Marcus's plan would show on me, like a smudge, but Grandpa merely nodded once. "Good night," he said.

"Good night."

I climbed the ladder to the loft and lay down. I hadn't slept well in weeks, but my eyes didn't want to close.

I wrapped my arms around my pillow, trying to quiet the confusion in my mind. Why should I be so upset about Grandpa and Darla? I imagined them together, Grandpa laughing at her jokes instead of ignoring them, looking her in the eye instead of away. Would he take her to Shadow Falls to teach her to climb, or would he want to keep her safe?

I made myself remember instead the feel of Marcus's hand squeezing mine as we'd said goodbye in Grandpa's driveway. He'd been soft, warm, caring. There was real goodness in him, a solid character that shone through his anger and frustration. He loved his brother as much as Cody had loved me. Maybe more. I didn't know what would happen between us, wasn't sure I needed to. I knew I wanted to be with him again, feel him near, his arms around me. I played it over and over in my mind.

Through the patterned sounds of the summer night I heard a tribe of coyotes cooing to each other in the darkness. I listened to their melody until I finally fell asleep.

18

The rhythm of the forest courses through my veins. The scent of the timber and the softness of the grass are my scent and my softness. I don't know where or what I am until the breeze carries a hint of sour flesh.

I am the grizzly.

I follow a trace of scent into the forest.

The morning is gentler. My forest is changing. With my claws I tear at new flowers. With my jaws I snap at the birds. I have not granted that this forest may grow.

The smell is strong and stings my nostrils like turpentine. The curtain of trees subsides, fails.

Once again, I stand in this meadow where the cruel shadows fall.

He is here.

He is standing with his back to me, wearing that orange vest. Slowly, he begins to turn toward me.

I can't look.

My hide stings. It itches with unbearable ferocity. I tear at my flesh with my claws. Blood pours over the new grass. The meadow blackens. I gouge at my legs and belly, chewing away my flesh.

Sickening flight, I fall up.

I am clinging to a branch high above the ground. My own remains are far beneath me, a pile of coarse brown fur, claws and teeth at the foot of the tree where I hide. My white skin is sticky with the blood of the grizzly, and it chills me as it dries. Twigs and dust plaster my matted hair. The rough bark of the tree gouges my white feet, but I wrap my toes around the branch and hug the prickly trunk. Where has my strength gone? I'm nothing but a weak girl. I'm so weak. "Don't say anything," I plead. From the safety of my tree I look into the meadow.

He is looking at me. His skin is rotten and gray, wretched with holes. His eyes are dried raisins. The breeze collides with him and works a lock of his hair loose from his scalp. The hair twirls in the wind, careening like a feather.

The branch under me begins to break.

And I am screaming, "I want to be with you!"

Turning, I am falling into the cavern, the deep stinking cave of Cody's open mouth where the black of his death awaits me. I sail into the dark where all the air is the wind and the wind is Cody's rotten voice howling:

"I will always be with you."

19

Someone is here. I knew this even before my nostrils burned with the scent of smoke threading through pines.

I stopped to listen. Nothing. I was on the path, about to round the bend that led to the Tepee Tree. I was probably just smelling a forest fire. I'd heard about one near Dubois, near enough for the wind to carry the smoke.

But the wind wasn't coming from the north.

I shifted the strap on my backpack and walked on, more slowly.

It was Saturday, a day off from watching Zachary. I'd waked from my dreams into terrified fury. Every fiber of every muscle screamed to be outside, so I'd written Grandpa a note and slipped out at the first spark of dawn. I'd been walking for over an hour in the dense part of the forest, sweating off the remains of that horrible dream. I felt safer on the trails than in my own bed.

Until I smelled the smoke again.

Someone is here. This time I knew for sure.

I stopped again to listen. I was standing where the

trail opened into the meadow, right next to the Tepee Tree.

Then I heard it. A voice meandered through the branches of Cody's hideout. No melody, no words, only a vague rhythm. The branches were dense, so I tilted my head until I found a chink to look through.

A man was sitting on the ground, slumped over the coals of a tiny fire. Draped over him was a heavy wool blanket—madness in the already thick heat of the day. His hair was matted, strewn with pine needles and twigs, and it hung in gray clumps. He swayed back and forth in time with his song. Or was it a prayer? A chant? He threw back his head and lifted his eyes to the lattice of branches above him.

I gasped. It was the old Indian man from Nora's Fish Creek Inn. What was he doing here?

His face was pale, and his lips were cracked. He looked sick.

His singing stopped.

His eyes were on mine.

He'd spotted me through the gap in the branches. I nearly turned to run, but his gaze softened and he smiled at me. He nodded and beckoned me with a hard brown hand. I shook my head at him, but he only chuckled weakly and beckoned me again. With rounded-out vowels and bitten-off consonants he said, "I've been waiting for you."

The scene had quickly gone from weird to utterly surreal.

I looked at him apprehensively. He was all hard-ened leather, yet his skin was so supple that the tiniest expression in his eyes changed the whole aspect of his face. He kept smiling. "We have something in com-mon. The grizzly, no? Sit down." He indicated a spot next to him and waited.

As I considered what to do, a deep instinct in me

surfaced, and I inexplicably understood that I could trust him. He had a comforting way of being strong and old, wise and innocent, quiet and completely present. And he had invited me to join him.

I eased through the tree branches and sat next to him on the ground.

He studied me in a posture of camaraderie. Then, satisfied, he turned and opened a roughly made deer-skin pouch and pulled out a pipe made from the antler of an antelope. It was beautiful, with blue and red beads twined around it on a thick cord, and leather tassels hanging from the end. He held it lovingly as he stuffed it with stringy, rich-smelling tobacco. He pushed the pipe over to me and handed me a book of matches. "I don't smoke," I said.

He grinned. "Neither do I." He put the end of the pipe to his mouth and struck a match. Holding the flame over the bowl of the pipe, he sucked vigorously until the tobacco glowed orange. Then, firmly, he handed me the pipe again.

"Hurry," he said, "before it burns out."

I tried to mimic the way he drew on the pipe, not in-haling the smoke, only pulling it into my mouth and pushing it back out again. Still, I coughed and gagged, and my vision got a little blurry. I handed it back to him, still hacking. He knocked the rest of the burning leaves into his fire and neatly tucked his pipe into the leather pouch.

I was smoking with a mysterious Indian next to a fire burning dangerously close to a very dry tree.

Grandpa would be delighted.

The man just sat there staring at me, bleary-eyed. I thought he might be waiting for me to say something. "So, uh, it's good to see you again," I offered.

He nodded once.

"Is this some kind of . . . vision quest?"

"None of your business."

I was taken aback, but he was grinning at me in a friendly way. "I'm sorry," I said, though I didn't understand what I'd done wrong.

"Indians don't like to talk about our religion." He shrugged. "It's personal."

"Okay." I felt sheepish. I leaned back on one hand and stared into the fire. Sweat collected above my eyebrows. He just sat there, staring ahead. "It's kind of hot with this fire," I observed astutely.

"I know," he intoned.

He seemed woozy. His eyelids kept drooping, and then his whole body would jolt and he would force them open again.

The oddness of the situation started to sink in. I figured I'd waited politely long enough. "Did you say you were expecting me?"

"It's personal." He tapped my knee with his fingertips, leaving a round, pink spot in my skin.

This frightened me. "You know"—I swallowed to stiffen my quivering voice—"I was kind of on my way somewhere."

He started swaying back and forth again, murmuring his haunting melody.

I looked at him in dumb shock. What exactly was I supposed to do here? He was ignoring me now, so I decided I'd had enough. I stirred, trying to get up, but he opened one eye at me and shook his head. I paused again. There wasn't anything about him that was threatening, but it didn't feel like a good place to be anymore. As quietly as I could, I situated my feet under me so that I'd be able to stand quickly and quietly. I waited there, squatting, watching him, looking for my chance to leave.

His voice grew louder and he waved his arms, but his movements were loose and weak.

"He's here," he muttered.

"What?" I looked at his face. He'd opened his eyes and fixed them on some point hovering in the air. "Are you okay?" I asked, but he didn't hear me. Lightly, I touched his shoulder.

As my hand grazed the wool of his blanket, something in him began to bend. His eyes rolled and his head flopped backward. Slowly, in minute stages, he sagged to the ground. He moaned loudly, his head lolling; his legs, awkward and limp, sprawled and kicked the coals of the fire.

"Oh my God. Sir?" I kicked at his leg until it moved away from the flames. The man didn't stir. "Can you hear me?" I shook him more roughly. "Sir! Sir!" He was completely unconscious. I gulped down panic. He might have simply passed out from the heat, but what if he'd had a stroke or a heart attack? He could die.

I ripped the wool blanket off him. With panicked fingers, I unbuttoned his sweaty shirt to cool him off. "You're going to be okay, sir," I said. "I'm going to get help. Don't worry." I was glad he couldn't hear me because there was nothing but fear in my voice.

I kicked dirt on the fire, then remembered my canteen and poured the water over the flames. I couldn't move fast enough. I fought through the branches of the trees, ignoring the scratches on my arms and neck. I found the trail and started running.

Please let Grandpa be home.

I ran the whole way to the cabin, but it still took me twenty minutes to get there.

When Grandpa saw me burst through the bushes, he dropped his book on the porch. "What happened?" He whisked me inside before I could get a word out. I was breathing too hard to talk.

"I'm okay. The old man . . ." A spasm of coughing took over my body, and I bent over with my hands on my knees, overcome. Grandpa poured me a glass of water, which I gulped down. Finally, I could speak. "In the woods. We have to go help him. I'll tell you on the way." I hurried out the door with Grandpa right behind.

We walked at a fast clip through the forest while I told Grandpa what happened. I wanted to run, but every time I sped up, Grandpa grabbed my elbow, saying, "You won't help him by getting heatstroke."

It was almost an hour later when we finally got to the Tepee Tree. "Sir! I'm back!" I tore through the branches and fell to the ground, looking around.

The old man was gone.

"Are you sure this is the spot?" Grandpa asked.

"Yes! This is his fire!"

"Where is he?"

"I don't know!" My voice was shrill.

Grandpa surveyed the ground. "Was he bleeding when you found him?"

"What?"

He pointed to a rusty patch next to where the man had been sitting. He knelt and picked up some of the moist, red dirt, breaking it between his fingers. "Yup. This is blood."

"Blood?" Now I was really freaking out. "When I left he was just unconscious!" I peered through the branches for a sign of him.

Grandpa scanned the ground, his eyes moving over the dirt and pine needles until they rested on one spot. The way his face froze made me stop breathing.

Grandpa was scared—scared like the day we met the grizzly on the river.

He crawled over to the edge of the trees, touched the ground with his fingertips, then looked above at the branches. Wisps of brown hair were clinging to a twig.

"Bear found him."

I focused my eyes on the top layer of dirt. Here and

there I saw faint claw marks and paw prints, superimposed on each other, near where the old man had lain. Grandpa clenched my arm. "You stay behind me, Annie. We're going to walk quickly, so keep alert." He hunched down to peer through the branches around us as he led me to the edge of the green canopy. "If you see a bear I want you up the nearest tree as fast as you can."

We kicked through the brush to the trail and Grandpa looked around to get his bearings. "We're only about a half mile from Darla's cabin," he said. "We'll go there."

We started off at a slow trot. Grandpa's stride was stiff and measured as he puffed up the trail. I followed behind, scanning everything for signs of a grizzly.

After a quarter mile, Grandpa stopped. At his foot was a huge bear track, carved into the packed clay of the trail. "We're following the bear, and the bear's following him." He pointed up ahead to rusty red drops strung along the side of the trail in an uneven curve. He ran the palm of his hand over his hair. My fear deepened as I realized he didn't know what to do. "We might surprise the bear, but five minutes on this trail will bring us right to Darla's." He looked at me, reading my face as though waiting for a suggestion.

I asked, "Well, how long ago were they here, do you think?"

"Blood's almost dry. I'd say—I don't know—maybe forty minutes?"

I noticed the breeze move across my cheek. "Well, if the bear's ahead of us, we're upwind of him. He can smell us already, probably, so we won't surprise him. . . ." I thought for a minute about backtracking, but what if the man was just ahead and needed our help? "Let's go to Darla's. We'll be able to get to a phone faster."

We crept along, our eyes moving over every branch and blade of grass around us. The bear tracks were steady and unfaltering as they paralleled the thin blood trail.

I felt Grandpa's hand tighten on my wrist and looked where he was pointing.

Ahead of us, on the path, lay the man's wool blanket, streaked with blood. A little ahead of that lay his leather pouch.

If my throat hadn't seized up, I might have screamed.

Grandpa tugged on my arm and broke into a run, pulling me along behind him, past the things scattered on the ground. I couldn't look in enough directions at once. As the trees broke and Darla's aspen grove appeared, Grandpa pushed me ahead of him. We bounded onto the porch, not bothering to knock, and catapulted ourselves into the cabin with a bang.

After rolling to a stop, I looked up to see Darla sitting at her immaculate kitchen table, pretty as you please in a blue sundress. She half stood and stared at Grandpa with her mouth open. "What a fright!"

With her, sipping tea from her English china and eating ladyfingers, sat the old man.

20

Darla smiled cheerily as though there were nothing out of the ordinary about serving afternoon tea to a wounded shaman. "Jack McGraw, please meet my very dear friend and colleague, Professor Joseph Rivers, Doctor of Philosophy in comparative religion. Anna, I believe that you two are already acquainted."

"You *know* this guy?" Grandpa asked, forgetting his manners.

"Joseph has been in the valley all summer without once calling me," Darla said indignantly. "I thought it might have been him you'd seen in the restaurant." As she spoke, she was applying butterfly adhesives to a gash on Joseph's shoulder, pulling the skin together before gingerly placing the white paper strips to close it. The old man, shirtless, sat tranquilly as four bright red lines of blood soaked through the gauze bandage taped to his chest.

I'd been so scared that once I was safe, I felt a little dizzy. I had to sit down, and I placed my palm flat on the cool Formica of the kitchen counter to steady myself.

Joseph leaned against the table, exhausted but content, as he poured himself another cup of tea and took a handful of cookies. One dropped on the floor and crumbled. Painfully he bent to sweep it up, but Darla slapped at his hand and knelt to do it herself. He seemed out of place at a table surrounded by comfortable things. He was rough and wild; he belonged in the forest.

"Pleased, to, uh . . ." Grandpa eased himself into one of the chairs and stared at Joseph, who looked right back at him, unperturbed. They sat like that in a stalemate until Grandpa finally hinted, "Were those bear tracks I saw with yours, Joseph?"

Grandpa usually isn't one to tiptoe around a question. Something about Joseph set him off-kilter. I couldn't blame him. Judging from the blood that was slowly penetrating the gauze on his chest, the man must be in real pain, but he seemed completely at peace. His strange calm unsettled me, too.

As if he hadn't even heard Grandpa's question, Joseph sat chewing his cookie, looking at no one, a slight smile bending his mouth. He swallowed, took a sip of tea from Darla's delicate china, patted at his lips with a linen napkin, and finally pointed in my direction. "Your granddaughter knows," he said.

I shook my head. "No. The bear must've come after I left."

Joseph nodded. "You brought me the power dream."

And I was back in my own dream, strolling through the forest in the thick hide of a bear. Every scent, every sensation, every thought was the grizzly's.

He nodded. "You brought me the message I was looking for." His eyes glistened with a grin. He folded his arms over his chest, taking care not to jostle his wound, and waited for me to respond.

Everyone was waiting.

I stammered. "J-Joseph, I didn't scratch you."

The twinkle in his eye turned to mirth.

"He's teasing you, dear." Darla patted my arm again. "Joseph loves his metaphors."

"How about you tell us what happened." Grandpa said this like a command. Joseph did not respond.

"We all want to hear what happened," Darla interjected, a little too lightly. "But first I need to make sure you don't get an infection." To Grandpa and me, she explained, "I can't talk Joseph into going to a doctor for a simple tetanus shot, much less stitches." She shook her head at him. "Really, Joseph, you're much too old to be taking risks like this."

Impassively, he swallowed some more tea. "I don't like doctors," he said in his gravelly English.

Darla scoffed. "He's afraid of needles. Always has been." From a small metal first-aid kit she produced a hypodermic and a tiny vial. "Too bad for you, I happen to have some penicillin right here." Joseph groaned. "Stop whining. I've done this a million times in the field." She plunged the needle through the membrane that sealed the medicine. Joseph bit his lip until it turned white. "How's Edna?" Darla asked, trying to distract him. "I haven't seen her since last summer."

Joseph looked at Darla hesitantly. "I don't know," he uttered quietly.

Darla was dabbing alcohol on his arm, but she looked up, surprised at his answer. She started to ask something but stopped herself. "You remember how accident-prone Winston was?" she said, changing the subject. "He was always coming home with some sort of wound from being careless on the dig." Without hesitation, Darla mercilessly sank the needle deep into his arm. Joseph winced, and a tear slid down his cheek. Hurriedly, he wiped it away, but not before Grandpa had raised an eyebrow. "Once, in Pakistan, he had a gash in his leg the length of his shinbone from falling on a shovel. I had to stitch him up. We had no anesthesia, but there were great amounts of vodka." She withdrew the needle and quickly pressed a cotton pad to the puncture. "Winston could handle needles."

"But not his vodka," Joseph added.

Darla gave him a pat on the shoulder, then sat down with a slender hand fitted into the crook of my grandfather's arm. "Now, Joseph, why don't you try telling us what happened in plain language? For novelty's sake."

He ignored Darla's tone, and paused to compose his thoughts. The room seemed to grow dimmer as he drew in breath to begin his story. "Usually dreams are just normal, everyday fantasies, but in my religion, some dreams can mean more. I call these power dreams." My nightmares of the black forest in mind, I leaned toward Joseph so I wouldn't miss anything. His speech was hushed, his gaze seemed focused on images from the past. "For me, power dreams are usually about grizzly bears. There is something about the grizzly spirit that calls to my dream self. Sometimes the dreams come to me in my sleep, like when the grizzly told me to go to Korea to become a soldier. I learned a lot in Korea." He pointed to a round scar just below his collarbone, about the size of a quarter. "Whenever I come to the end of a path and I don't know where to take up again, I often feel the need to test myself. I do this when I've made mistakes, to ask for guidance."

Grandpa shifted in his chair uneasily, and Joseph turned to look at him. "When I saw your granddaughter in the restaurant and I heard that the grizzly had kissed her, I took it as confirmation I would find my message here in this valley where my grandfather used to come for visions. Still, I was confused. Why would the grizzly work through a white child?"

I saw Grandpa stiffen. "I'm one-eighth Blackfoot," I blurted, to keep him quiet.

Joseph raised his eyebrows as he studied my features. "Yes, now I see." I shifted so that a lock of hair hung in my face. He went on, "Still, she is a strange one for the grizzly spirit. She is too small, and only a girl."

Darla snorted angrily. "Really, Joseph!"

"For a while I behaved like an old woman who only knows how to complain."

Darla huffed again.

His eyes twinkled with the pleasure of getting Darla's goat. "I went to a powerful part of the forest with no water or food, and I sat without moving for two days and two nights to wait for a power dream. But still, none came. On the third day, when I was very, very thirsty and very hot, I saw your granddaughter peeking at me through the branches of the tree, with her small face and her brown eyes and brown hair, like a bear cub. Maybe this was just coincidence, but it seemed significant, so I shared my tobacco with her, even though"—he glanced wryly at Darla—"she is only a woman."

I felt my face get hot and might have said something myself if Darla hadn't snapped, "Get to the point, Joseph."

"We smoked my pipe and we waited until finally my dream came. I fell on the ground, and the sun became close to me and very hot. Your granddaughter stripped my chest to the air. And then her face grew long, her body grew fat and large, her fingers turned to claws, and then she was a grizzly. She slashed my chest and made me bleed. She spoke to me. Then the bear left, dragging my pipe sack with it. I thought this meant I should follow, and I did."

Grandpa broke in. "You mean *you* were following *the grizzly*?"

Joseph looked at him in surprise. "You thought the bear was following me?"

Grandpa nodded.

"Well, then, you're not a very good tracker."

Grandpa opened his mouth to take exception, but Darla interrupted. "What did the bear tell you, Joseph?"

"None of your business."

"Give us *something*," she said.

Joseph looked right at me. "Sometimes people wander a long time in the woods, lost because they don't notice the signs around them." He slowly sat back in his chair, a punctuation for the end of his story. His eyes remained on mine.

Grandpa looked at Darla, and then at me, clearly thinking Joseph was a complete wacko. Darla ignored Grandpa and nodded at Joseph, looking at him solemnly as though he were a priest who'd just delivered a sermon. When I looked again at Joseph, he was still staring at me, appraising but kind.

I'd never believed in anything unseen. There were no ghosts or demons or angels, and if there was a God, he seemed aloof at best. Besides, my eyes showed me everything I needed, which was why I loved photography. It forced me to live in the moment I was trying to capture. To get good pictures I had to really look at the world around me instead of losing myself in my thoughts. Because if you're looking at what's in front of you while thinking about something else, you just end up seeing the shadow your own mind casts over the world.

My eyes were drawn back to the tawny light of Joseph's gaze. I thought about how the fibers of his story extended into the weave of my dreams. Maybe there was more to the world than I could see through my camera after all. I glanced out Darla's kitchen window, crazily expecting to see the charred remains of an incinerated forest, but the aspens were shimmering silver and green in the breeze.

Darla wordlessly got up and filled a glass with water,

then handed it to Joseph with two pills. "Not a word from you about how you don't like pills. This is an anti-inflammatory and you absolutely must take it." He grudgingly swallowed them. Darla stood over him with her arms folded across her chest. "Now you listen to me, old man. You are going to stay with me until I am absolutely certain that you won't develop an infection." Joseph opened his mouth to protest, but Darla stamped her foot. She pointed her finger to the kitchen door and bellowed, "Now you *get* into the bathroom and *clean* yourself up, and then go *peacefully* into my bedroom and go to sleep!"

Joseph struggled to his feet. "I think the bear dropped my bag on the trail." He glanced around. "And my blanket—I must have dropped it."

"Jack will get them for you. Now go wash up, but keep your wounds dry."

Joseph stretched himself to his full height. Next to tiny Darla, he seemed a giant, almost as tall as Grandpa. But she held her ground, jutting her chin at him stubbornly, her gray eyes unwavering. Finally, looking a little defeated, he limped out of the kitchen, muttering over his shoulder, "I will stay five days."

Darla got up to clear the dishes. "Jack, can you hand me those cups and saucers?"

I watched as Grandpa got up from the table to take Joseph's plate to the sink. He leaned toward Darla and looked at her tenderly as he put the dish under the water. She glanced at him, then tilted her head toward his shoulder without touching it. Grandpa was so soft toward her, gentle and caring.

"Go have a lie-down on my sofa, dear. Your grandfather and I can manage this." I got up to try to help, but she firmly refused. "No, Anna. You should rest yourself." She handed me a big glass of water.

I was actually glad to have an excuse to leave. I didn't want to be alone with them anymore.

The living room was cooler than the kitchen, though the sun shone brightly through Darla's lace curtains. I was still jumpy from all the excitement, so I paced the room, looking again at the photos of Bion. He looked very young in his graduation photo compared with some of the other pictures. In one he was standing in front of a bright blue tent, his pale skin weathered and freckled, his lips pale and cracked from being in the sun too much.

"He was a good boy."

I turned to see Joseph standing behind me. "What happened to him?"

"He died of a fever in Sudan four years ago while studying the Dinka people there. He gave away all his medicine, and when he got sick, he had none for himself."

"That's horrible," I said, thinking about Darla's determined strength. Somehow, she'd managed to move on. I didn't think I would ever be able to get over losing Cody if I had a million years to do it. "Poor Darla."

He nodded solemnly. "It was a good death."

I had no idea what he meant by that, but the idea of a "good" death was offensive to me. I said nothing.

"I wanted to talk to you alone." He smiled mysteriously and slowly lowered himself onto the sofa, wincing a little before he settled into the cushions. "So many coincidences. I come to this valley, this sacred place, looking for a message from Great-Grandfather. I find you talking in the restaurant about bears. Then I'm in the woods waiting for a power dream and you find me. And then the bear comes. It's strange, isn't it?" His expression seemed faintly amused, but his eyes were serious.

I was silent. The whole thing was so freaky, I wasn't sure I wanted to discuss it.

He seemed to tire of waiting for me to speak. With a smirk, he looked me up and down. "You are like a mouse who knows a hawk sees her, but stays still pretending to be a rock," he said. "I didn't recognize the grizzly in you."

"Yeah, well"—I tried to laugh—"I'm a Taurus."

"Are you making fun of me?"

He seemed hurt, but I didn't care. He knew too much, seemed to see too much. And I was annoyed that he would call me a mouse. I stared right back into his tawny, pinpoint eyes. "I'm not a mouse," I said quietly.

He studied my unwavering gaze, then smiled at me warmly, nodding in assent. "I am sorry."

This appeased me for the moment. "Anyway, my mom says I'm more like an armadillo."

He lifted his eyebrows. "Yes, I see why. The armadillo is like the bear, a solitary animal." He held up his hands in a gesture of uncertainty. "Maybe you seem like an armadillo because you haven't accepted the grizzly inside you."

I looked at four bloody lines across his chest. "Why did he do that?"

"She."

"She?"

"The bear wandering this forest is a sow."

"Does it matter if it's a male or female?"

"Maybe humans make it matter more than it should." He sheepishly pointed his thumb toward the wound on his chest. "A she-bear can kill you just as dead as a boar." He shrugged, but the motion hurt him. He screwed his eyes shut, raising his hand to his chest. I realized again how much pain he must be in, and how little he showed it. After a few deliberate breaths, he said, "Darla told me your brother was a climber."

"Yes." It's a short word, but my clipped tone made it even shorter.

"Climbers are like eagles. They like to be high above the earth."

"I guess."

"Your brother also died well."

That got me angry again. "You've never even met my brother."

"No. But a person's death can say a lot about his life. He died trying to save others. That is a good death."

"Dead is dead." The pressure of tears strained my voice. I was sick of death. Sick of talking about death, thinking about death, dreaming about it. I hate death. It takes away everything, leaves nothing for you to hang on to.

I tried to hang on anyway. Six weeks after the phone call I went into Cody's room and looked through his dresser, trying to find some remnant of him that I could keep. I found a picture in his sock drawer of him with a girl I'd never met. She had green eyes and tan skin and chestnut hair, and Cody had his arm around her. He was holding a beer and they were both smiling big for the camera. They seemed so happy. I realized Cody had a whole life, entire experiences that I didn't know about. This girl might have been a friend or a date or a girlfriend—she meant enough to him that he kept her picture. Still, he never told me about her. Never even mentioned a girl. I realized that no matter how hard I tried to remember him, I was only remembering a piece of him, the part of him that was my big brother. So what people were constantly telling me, that as long as we remember him he would live on, was total bullshit. No matter how much I remembered him, the vibrant galaxy that had been Cody McGraw had become a black hole. It surrounded me every day but refused to swallow me up, and I just had to live inside the emptiness.

And now, here was Joseph, telling me his death had been good, that there was something noble about it. How dare he say that to me? "All the climbers died that day." I spat bitter words. "Cody's death didn't help anyone."

Joseph stared at me for a long time, weaving an in-explicable thread of shame into my anger. Quietly, he said, "He lost his life trying to save others. That is what brave men do. Give him the honor of having pride in that."

"Pride is nothing against grief."

"Pride is a duty, and a choice. You are failing your brother by insisting on the futility of his death. You are failing yourself."

"You don't know anything about me!" I squinted hard out the window to keep my tears from tumbling. If anyone had failed Cody, it was Grandpa. He was the one who had pushed Cody to fatal heights.

"You'll see." Joseph stood up, swooned a little, then regained his balance and started walking to the bed-room. "You only need time."

21

"Any more deviled eggs?" Marcus asked as he sat up too quickly, rocking the canoe.

"Watch out!" I yelled, sure we would capsize. He was no good in boats. "No sudden movements! And no! We're out."

He grabbed the sides of the boat but tried to look at ease. "Relax, will you?" he said, unsteadily, with a nervous smile.

I had foolishly thought we were going on a simple picnic, but when Marcus showed up that morning with a green fiberglass canoe strapped to the roof of his car, I knew we were in for trouble. "Isn't it great? I found it in Mabel's shed!" He told me he'd spent hours clearing out the spiderwebs and checking for leaks to make absolutely certain it was seaworthy. We'd unloaded it from the car, launched it, and let the weak current carry us to the middle of tiny String Lake. That's when we realized he'd forgotten the paddles. Now we were lying in the bottom of the boat, his head at one end, mine at the other, surrendering to sunburn.

I let my fingers trail in the chilly water. "One of us is

going to have to get in that water to push the boat back to shore," I said.

"I'll direct you from here."

"If you don't watch it, you'll be directing me from the middle of the lake."

"I love it when you discipline me," he said with a leer.

I giggled. "Cody used to call me Miss Bitchy Boss."

He seemed to fade into his own thoughts, but he suddenly turned to me, rocking the boat gently. "That's the first time you've ever brought him up."

I looked at him for a moment, then adjusted the rim of my ball cap to shade my eyes.

"You know, I talk to you about my mom and dad all the time," he reminded me.

It was true. Telling me his secret that night at Dornan's seemed to open a lock he'd kept on his thoughts and memories. Every time I'd seen him since, he'd told me more. His mom would get so drunk she wouldn't know what she was saying. She once told him, "You stink just like your father. Just like rotten cabbage." He said it wasn't even the worst thing she'd said, but it was what hurt him the most. He always told me these things with an even tone, his face blank. It seemed now he thought it was my turn to talk.

"I don't ever talk about him, really."

"Tell me." His voice was firm, his eyes like two brown river rocks.

I ducked my head even lower so the brim of my cap hid my face entirely. "Go fish."

"Tell me!" he insisted, then to emphasize his point he grabbed hold of the sides and started rocking us violently.

"Stop it! God! You're crazy!"

"I'll stop it when you tell me."

"All right!" He let go of the sides and the canoe

slowly quieted. I closed my eyes and consciously tried to loosen the knot in my throat. Could I tell him about Cody? Could I talk? "He was . . . great," I started. Marcus leaned back in the canoe, his eyes trailing the green water at his side. Now that he wasn't looking at me, it was easier. "He was my hero. He was . . . everything, I guess. Maybe he was for me what you are for Zachary, you know? He filled in for my dad, who I don't even know. Cody took care of me. I depended on him. That's why it hurt so much when Joseph said I was failing him." It had been almost two weeks since that conversation. I'd settled into a kind of routine. I didn't see Grandpa much anymore, which suited me just fine. I watched Zachary during the day and then spent evenings hanging out with Marcus. Through all this time, though, Joseph's words never entirely left my mind. I'd become obsessed. It was the last thing I thought about as my head hit the pillow, and if I was lucky enough to fall asleep, it seemed to echo through my dreams and into the birdsong that woke me up in the morning. *Failing him. Failing him. Failing him.*

"Who's Joseph?"

"That Indian. You know."

"Native American?"

"I think they prefer to be called Indians. Sherman Alexie does."

"Who?"

"He's a writer. A good writer. He's Spokane or Coeur d'Alene, I think."

"Anyway, how can you fail someone who isn't alive?"

"I don't know. Maybe—"

"Don't listen to that old blowhard." He waited for me to look at him; then he smiled. "Keep going. Tell me more about Cody."

I cast my eyes across the lake at the Tetons, which

were so close they seemed to be leaning backward, looking at the sky. "He had a great laugh. Right from deep down in his belly, and it would just sail over everyone's head and people would stop talking and look for where it was coming from. And he had beautiful eyes. Blue eyes. Light blue, like Grandpa's. I was the only one in our family who didn't get those eyes."

"Hey! What's wrong with brown?"

"Nothing," I said, really meaning it. I loved Marcus's brown eyes, how hard they could be one moment and soft the next. He smiled at me.

"You're not really going to leave with Zachary, are you?" I'd wanted to ask for a long time and was waiting for the moment. Now seemed right.

"Nah, I think I'll live out my days in this canoe," he said, leaning his head back so that the sun draped over him. "Tell me more about Cody."

"Well . . ." I looked at the white haze of clouds in the sky, soft tendrils of white threading through the breeze. I thought of something I wanted to say, but I felt shy. The armadillo defense was a hard habit to break, but with Marcus I didn't want to be an armadillo. "Actually, you remind me of my brother a little."

He pulled his head upright to look at me. "What do you mean?"

"I don't know. You're self-confident like him. And the way you walk, easy strides. He used to put one hand in his jeans pocket like you do, all the time. And you kind of laugh like him. Also, your arms. His were really strong, with really defined muscles and not much hair, like yours."

His eyes flicked over me warily as he said, "You don't sound like you're talking about your brother."

My cheeks flushed. "What do you mean?"

"You talk about him like he was your boyfriend or something."

I sat up. The canoe bucked, but I didn't care. "What are you trying to say?" I asked, my voice watery.

"It's just weird, is all." He folded his arms over his chest and kicked at the side of the boat with his sneaker. "I mean, why would you want to date someone who reminded you of your brother?"

If I hadn't been in the middle of a lake in a canoe with no paddle, I would have stormed away from him. "That's an unbelievably shitty thing to say."

"Don't get all mad, I didn't mean—"

"And who says we're dating?"

"I thought we—"

"You're implying that I—I don't even want to say what you're implying!" I slapped the water with my hand a few times, watching the angry droplets careen away.

"I don't mean to. It's just, it weirds me out a little."

"You asked! You practically pried it out of me!"

"Not every guy is thrilled to learn he reminds a girl of her brother, you know?" He turned one palm up as though he were trying to reason with someone who was very very slow.

"Cody was a great person. I meant that as a compliment to you!"

"Well, it didn't feel like one."

I had to stand or I would explode. Quickly, without even thinking about it, I stripped down to my swimsuit, jumped into the lake and swam for shore. The water was achingly cold, but it was better than staying in the canoe with Marcus.

Marcus lamely paddled with his hands, calling, "Calm down, Annie! Stop, will you? Just come back!"

My fury grew with every stroke. I put everything I was feeling into swimming—the anger, the indignation. The shame. I swam so fast I made it to shore sooner than I could have run there. I started to walk toward the parking lot, thinking I'd hitch a ride, but realized all my clothes were in the canoe and I didn't even have any shoes, so instead I sat on a big crooked tree stump, letting the sun dry me out. A couple of little kids were chasing after minnows down the shoreline, and I could hear their parents calling, "Only out to your waist!" They stopped to stare when Marcus tooled up, cupping his hands in the water on either side of the canoe for makeshift paddles. He looked pathetic. Finally he got to the shallows and jumped out of the boat, pulling it behind him until he could wedge it into the coarse sand on the shore. He stopped at the edge of the water and looked at me meekly.

"Are you going to unman me with that swimmer's kick?"

"Shut up."

"You're overreacting."

"You're a jerk."

"I'm not a jerk."

"You are."

"Come on. Let's not fight, okay?" Slowly he came over to me, his hands deep in the pockets of his jeans. He sat down behind me on the stump. I tried to lean away, but he wrapped his arms around me and held me so that I had to lean into him. I felt his breath on my skin and warmth seeped through me. I melted a little. "I didn't mean it that way," he murmured.

You sound like you're talking about your boyfriend. How many ways could he have meant it? "Take it back."

"I take it back."

"Say you're sorry."

"I never meant it like that."

"Say you're *sorry*," I insisted. I was trapped by his arms, his hands on my skin, his hip pressing against mine. I felt divided in two halves—the hurt, angry half who wanted an apology, and the half who realized I was close to him wearing only a swimsuit. "I mean it. Apologize," I said, fighting down the sensation of his skin on mine.

"I shouldn't have to apologize if I didn't mean it like that."

That made me even madder. I burst out of his hold, got up from the stump and marched away without even thinking where I intended to go. I had kicked into the water up to my knees before I turned around to face him. "Jerk!" I shouted. The little kids stopped playing in the water and started walking toward their parents, their wide eyes on us. For the first time in my life, I was angry enough not to care that I was making a scene. "You owe me an apology!"

"Okay! Okay!" He got up from the rock and took two steps toward me, laughing a little. He seemed to think I was funny, and that only made me angrier.

"I mean it!"

"You're right." He sobered up and slowly started walking toward me. I thought he would stop when he reached the border of the water, but he didn't. He strode into it, shoes, jeans and all, and didn't stop until he was nearly touching me. "I'm sorry, Annie."

I folded my arms. "Apologize again."

"I'm sorry." He put his hands on my shoulders and gently shook me. His sad eyes traveled over every surface of my face to finally rest on my lips. Again he whispered, "I am. I'm sorry."

"Jerk," I whispered, but my heart was racing. I leaned away from him, trying to hang on to the Annie who was mad, who demanded an apology, but the Annie in the swimsuit slowly took over, and as he softly brushed his lips over mine, I finally leaned in to put my head on his shoulder, telling myself, *He didn't mean it. He didn't mean it that way.*

22

I entered the cabin slowly, already sore from the monster sunburn I'd gotten at the lake. It was already dark, but instead of quizzing me about Marcus like he'd been doing every night that week, Grandpa reminded me to call Mom.

I picked up the phone as though it were a court subpoena and held the antenna in my teeth as I scaled the ladder to the loft. I missed her, but I felt like even when I was talking to her, we were both thinking about something else. It wasn't that she didn't try. She would ask me all the questions she always asked me. "How was your day? . . . How's it going with Grandpa? . . . Is Zachary doing better?" But she didn't seem to care about the answers. It seemed like she was dispensing with the required duties so she could go back to being devastated.

The phone rang six times before she picked it up.

"Mom, it's Annie."

"You're calling late, sweetie. Where have you been?"

"Out."

"With whom?"

"Marcus."

"You're seeing a lot of him lately."

"Yes." My voice sounded rigid. I could sense some "straight talk" coming.

"You like him?"

I thought about what he'd said to me in the canoe. I'd finally opened up to him and he made me feel like a freak. I wasn't sure anymore how I felt about him, especially once I was away from him, where he couldn't smooth over his rough remarks by touching me. Still, I knew for sure I didn't want to talk about it with Mom. "Yeah. I like him."

"You don't sound sure."

"I am."

"Your grandfather thinks he's a rather troubled boy, Annie."

"He's a good person."

"You're hardly spending any time with Grandpa, though."

I shot a look down at him. He was sitting at the kitchen table pretending to do a crossword, but he seemed to have one ear trained on me. "He has Darla."

"Yeah, from what he tells me, it sounds kind of serious."

"It's gross," I said, making no effort to speak quietly. He flicked his eyes at the floor, then back to his paper.

"I think it's wonderful. He's been alone far too long."

"Well," I said, trying to find a different tack. I'd hoped she would feel the same way I felt about it, and this was disappointing. "He's with her a lot."

"Annie!" She let loose half a giggle. "You sound jealous!"

"Well, I'm not," I said sharply. But what if it was true?

Could it be that I was jealous of Darla? What kind of freak was I?

"Are you"—Mom paused as if trying to decide whether to dive into cold water—"getting physical with Marcus?" she finally asked.

"Oh God, Mom."

"Tell me."

"Nothing major," I said, even though what was happening with Marcus felt major to me.

"Is he your boyfriend?"

"I don't know." I'd never even been on a date with anyone before Marcus, and I realized I had no idea what I was to him. I wished I could ask Cody how you tell if a guy really likes you, but then I wondered if I would really talk to Cody about this. Would I keep it a secret from him, just like he'd hidden the green-eyed girl from me?

"Just be careful, Annie."

"I am, Mom."

"Boys are tricky. You have no idea."

"Okay."

She sighed. "I used to worry about you less when Cody was around to look out for you."

I sat there pressing the phone into my ear. For the first time in months, Mom had summoned Cody's horrible absence by uttering his name. Did this mean it was finally okay to talk about him? "Mom, remember when I was little and I wanted to marry Cody?"

"Yes. Of course." She made a sound somewhere between a chuckle and a sob. "You used your Snow White pillowcase for a veil."

I swallowed down the lump in my throat. Marcus had made me feel so bad, so dirty. "Do you think that's weird?"

She was silent for a second. "Weird?"

"Am I a freak?"

"Oh, honey, no. No, you're not. You idolized Cody. You loved him. You were a tiny little thing back then, sweetie. You didn't know."

"But maybe—" Now the tears were running away from me, and I couldn't stop them. "Maybe there's something wrong with me."

"Honey, it's perfectly, absolutely normal."

"Is it?"

"When Cody was four he proposed marriage to me!"

"Really?"

"You had no daddy to attach to, Annie." She spoke consolingly, warmly. She sounded like my mom again for a second. "Cody was it for you."

"Yeah," I whispered. I pressed my hand over my eyes and held it there, as if the pressure could steady my voice. "My dad was part Indian, right?"

"Yes, he was."

"Did he"—I closed my eyes and saw the shadow of a bear in the dark of my lids—"believe in any Indian stuff ever?"

"Indian stuff?"

"I've been having these really bad dreams. About bears. And Cody's there."

Her voice was barely there. "I have nightmares too."

"I'm just mad at him, you know?"

"Who?"

"Cody, for taking chances like he did."

"Yeah," she said carefully, as though her voice were balanced on the sharp end of a needle. "Me too."

"Why did you let Grandpa teach him to climb?" I spoke softly so he couldn't hear. "It's so dangerous, but Grandpa never seemed to care about that."

"Of course he cared!"

"Why did you let Cody go to Argentina?"

A long silence stretched all five hundred miles between us. "*Let* him?" she finally asked.

Suddenly the moment was over. I couldn't talk about it anymore. "It's late," I said.

She was silent for a long time before she finally whispered, "Okay."

After we hung up I buried my head under my pillow, thinking about my fight with Marcus. I was still angry, but I realized that, in a twisted way, he'd been right. It wasn't that I'd ever wanted Cody to be my boyfriend. I'd wanted Marcus to be Cody. I missed my brother so much, I'd tried to replace him.

I pressed the cool cotton pillow hard into my face, almost hard enough to smother.

23

*It's about one o'clock in the afternoon on a Tuesday.
I would be in biology class. You're with your friends at
camp on the south face of Aconcagua, the most difficult route in the Andes. You've been camped above
17,000 feet for only one night, but it's long enough that
you've forgotten how it feels if your nose isn't numb.
You're waiting in the shelter of your tent for the other
team to come back from the first attempt at the summit.*

*You're worried. You might have to leave before you
get your chance at the highest peak in the Americas.
One of the climbers above you has developed mild altitude sickness, so the first ascent team has turned back in
the hopes that Martin will get better. You're keeping
everyone's mind off the worry, though, if I know you.
Probably doing your stupid Willie Nelson impersonation
or something, keeping everyone laughing.*

*Suddenly, a charging rumble echoes through the
ridges of the peaks above you, and you all stop to listen. When the noise subsides, one of the climbers,
maybe it's you, lunges for the radio and frantically
starts calling up to the first ascent team. "Anyone up*

there? You guys okay? Hello?" You wait, all of you, for agonizing seconds, then minutes, in grave silence.

But finally, a voice comes through on the other end. "We got tipped by the edge of that slide! Martin's back is hurt." More terrible luck.

"Can you guys get him down?"

There's a frightening pause. Finally, the climber on the radio, probably Bill Morris, says simply, "He started throwing up."

You know what this means. The stress of the injury has aggravated Martin's altitude sickness. He's straight on the course toward a fatal blood clot, maybe in his lungs, maybe in his brain. The obvious solution is to get him down as quickly as possible, but there's a problem. At that elevation, it is virtually impossible for two men to quickly carry a third down a temperamental mountainside.

The choices are ugly. Let them take their chances and hope Martin makes it. Or go up to help them carry him down. If you go up, you would have to cross the huge Superior Glacier, which is where avalanches on this side of the mountain are born. One avalanche is often followed by another, especially in winds like this. It's a huge risk and you all know it.

But Martin's your buddy.

So you break camp as quickly as possible. You set off at a slow gait, which is all the speed you can manage in that empty air. You are probably in the lead because you're younger and stronger than anyone else, and you're such a damn show-off.

It's about four o'clock by now. I would be at home, fixing myself some chocolate milk. You're just meeting up with the other climbers beyond where the ice had raced its furious course. The group makes one last radio call to a team of Italian climbers so they can relay a message to the authorities asking for help.

If you hadn't done that, I would never have known what happened to you.

You've fixed Martin to his sled and you're all retracing your steps, just about to set off across that deadly glacier.

The snow is blinding. It's a clear day, and the sunlight warms you even though the air is so cold it seems to have frozen the howling of the wind. You're all plodding along, one leaden foot after another, forcing your pace. The thin air makes you feel as though your pack weighs five hundred pounds. You are utterly, completely, painfully exhausted.

The only sounds are the wind whipping your face and the rhythmic crunch of the snow under your boots.

Until you hear it. That low rumble of dynamite. You look up the mountainside at the snowy cloud descending upon you. It's so far away at first that it looks like it's moving slowly, and you think you can make it if you run. But you're above 19,000 feet. A single step is a superhuman feat of strength.

But you do it, Cody. You take off at a jog though your legs are screaming and your head is swimming. Maybe you're still trying to pull Martin on his sled. Maybe you have enough sense to drop the rope and leave him. Probably not, knowing you. I doubt the thought that you might not make it even crosses your mind.

Then it hits you. Tons of ice and snow with all the momentum it had gained traveling down one of the highest peaks on earth.

Maybe it kills you instantly.

Maybe you survive the initial impact. You try to swim in that great swirl of ice, moving your broken limbs to stay near the top of it. The noise is deafening. Your ears are probably bleeding. You can't tell which way is up. You're screaming but no one can help you. The icefall moves on furiously, carrying you to a place no one will ever find.

As suddenly as it started, the avalanche crushes to a halt.

Now it's about five o'clock in the afternoon. Mom is leaving the office, I'm sitting down to do my homework, and you're fighting to breathe. As strong as you are, there's so much weight that you can't open your ribs to let in any air. There's no air to be had.

The pain is simply unimaginable. You're right there feeling it, the frigid, constricting pressure on your arms, your legs, your ribs, your face, but it's so much pain you can't believe it's happening. If you could, you would groan, but all the air has been squeezed from your lungs. You're inert, as immovable as the ice that is crushing you.

And it's incredible, but all this is happening to you, and I have no idea. No psychic hint, no weird feeling, no premonition or nightmare or anything. It's just another night.

I imagine you lying in the darkness as you wait to die.

What do you think about? Do you think about Mom? Or Grandpa? Do you think about me? Do you imagine that last time we saw each other in Denver, just before you boarded the plane?

I doubt it.
You think about all the mountains you will never
    conquer.
You think about how sunlight makes granite sparkle
    like dew.
You think about the navy blue sky above the
    alpine line.
You imagine the sound of your own voice
        returning to you
            in an echo.

24

Zachary dumped his satchel on the floor of the kitchen, his forehead knit together like a tightly drawn net. Without even saying hello, he heaved himself onto the sofa, a huge book about the solar system in his lap, roughly flipping the pages.

I sat next to him and put my hand on his shoulder. "Zachary, is there anything wrong?" He jerked out from under my grasp and shook his head. "You can't fool me, Zachary. Something's bothering you."

His moist bottom lip drooped. "Everything is fine," he muttered.

"If you say so." I watched his big eyes move mechanically over the page in front of him. I was actually glad he didn't want to talk. I'd hardly slept the night before, too haunted by pictures of avalanches to close my eyes. I didn't have energy for Zachary's problems, too. "Can I read one of your books?"

He nodded, but made no move toward his purple satchel, so I sat down next to him and started to look through it. There were dozens of old candy bar wrappers inside the bag, and they rustled around in the bottom. For a skinny little kid, he sure ate a lot of chocolate. "You gonna build a nest with these?" I asked, thinking joking with him might help.

He ignored me.

I let out a long sigh through clenched teeth and looked at him sideways. I thought about leaving him be. It would certainly be easier—but maybe he'd been left too much. "Zachary, you know, what you're doing right now isn't helping. You're just shutting out someone who cares about you and wants to help."

His eyes stopped moving over the words in front of him and rose to the top of the page to rest there. He seemed to be listening.

"I think you should tell me what's wrong."

His jaw set. "Leave me alone," he said, but his eyes were steady. He was still listening to me.

"Tell me."

He clenched his fists and slammed them against his book. "I miss my mom, okay? Will you shut up and leave me alone, now? Just leave me alone!"

And suddenly he was wailing. He dropped his book on the floor and gave himself up to it. I put my arm around him, and he slowly let himself lean against me. I fumbled for something to say. "It'll be okay . . . Go ahead and cry." I wrapped myself around him, instinctively trying to shield him even though the violence of his despair frightened me.

It was a long time before he finally quieted down. I handed him a tissue. "Feel a little better now?"

He nodded as he dabbed at his tears. His nose was running, so I took another tissue and wiped it for him. "Maybe you just needed a good cry."

He nodded. "Don't tell Marcus I cried, okay? Even though you are best friends? Because you are my best friend too, okay?"

For the first time ever, I gave Zachary a kiss on the forehead, and for the first time, he didn't shrink from my touch. "I promise I won't tell a soul, Zachary." His face was blotchy and red from crying, his eyes hooded by dark circles. He looked exhausted. "Did something happen to make you so upset, Zachary?"

He turned toward the window. "Mabel asked me last night if I wanted to live with her."

"But you want to go back and live with your mom?"

Tears threatened again, but he took in a deep gust of breath. "I like staying with Grandma," he said. "She cooks supper and reads me stories and tucks me in. It's easier with Grandma, but I still miss Mommy."

"I know."

"Is she going to call me today?"

"She said she would."

His gaze faded as he considered something. "Do you think Grandma will hate me if I want to go back home?" he finally asked.

"Of course not, Zachary. Everyone loves you."

He chewed on his lip thoughtfully. "Marcus hates Grandma."

"I don't think that's really true, Zachary."

"Yes, it is. He said it this morning because they had a fight. It's stupid, because they spell words they think I don't understand."

"Like what?"

"Like *trial* and *custody* and *adopt*. Those words are easy." He shook his head.

"They probably don't know what an amazing reader you are."

He stared at his feet for a while. "Things would be easier if Marcus wasn't so mad."

"At Mabel?"

He scoffed. "Marcus is mad at everyone."

He was right. Marcus could be sweet one minute and turn on you the next. I'd learned that much on our canoe trip. "Yeah, but he's not mad at you."

"He tells me to shut up a lot."

"Yeah, well, he's your big brother."

"So?"

"I think that's kind of how big brothers act."

"Did your brother tell you to shut up too?"

"Yep, he did."

"Your big brother is dead, right?"

I couldn't speak. I nodded.

"My mom almost died."

"I know." My voice sounded pebbly like the bottom of the Snake River.

"I saved her life." He puffed out his chest. His mouth smiled, but he still looked sad. "I called Marcus at work when I saw her and the ambulance came."

"That must have been so awful, Zachary."

He nodded, his big brown eyes on mine as he said solemnly, "She was lying in throw-up."

He turned away to look at his shoes. It was awful to think he carried that image around with him. "But she made it," I reminded him. "You saved her."

"I know." He was quiet, wringing his little hands. He seemed to be concentrating hard. Finally he turned to me and asked, "Did you try to save your brother?"

The question turned me to stone. I stared at him, trying to think of an answer. But all I could do was tell the truth. I said no.

25

The next morning, Grandpa shook me awake with a big hand clamped on my shoulder. His voice was gruff. "It's almost eight."

Downstairs, I picked at my eggs. Grandpa watched me from under his thick eyebrows. I sank toward my plate when I saw him looking at me. "It's been a while since you and I have gotten out, Annie," he said, "Why don't we take the boat on the river?"

Dreading the thought of a full day alone with Grandpa, I pondered which would be more believable, a fake headache or a fake sore throat. We both started when the phone rang, and I jumped up to grab it.

"It's me, Marcus." He spoke in a low, intimate tone that made me blush. "It looks like the big day is coming sooner than we thought."

I huddled away from Grandpa and whispered, "What big day?"

"I promised I would call before we left, so . . ."

I nearly dropped the phone. I hadn't believed Marcus would actually go through with it. "Hello?" Marcus said.

"Wait a second!" I shouted. Grandpa looked up

from the dishes he was gathering from the table. I forced my voice to a calmer range. "What happened?"

"Mom is trying to leave rehab early so she can take me and Zachary back home. Mabel's in town right now, meeting with a lawyer to try to stop her."

"Does Zachary know about this?"

"We'll be gone before Mabel has a chance to tell him."

"Marcus, this is crazy! You don't even know where to go, or—"

"I was thinking we could settle in Denver near you. Wouldn't that be cool?"

I was starting to feel nauseated. Live near me? I suddenly felt very young. "I didn't understand how serious you were!" I whispered.

"I just hope when we're gone, they realize what they've done."

Yesterday Zachary was sobbing on the couch because he was being torn in two different directions. I didn't want to see him torn in a third. "Marcus," I started gently, "maybe you should rethink this."

There was a pause. "What do you mean?"

I looked to make sure Grandpa wasn't listening. He had turned up the radio for the news and was washing dishes. "I think you should wait and see what happens between Mabel and your mom."

Again he paused. "I should never have told you," he snarled.

"Please don't say that."

"I thought I could trust you." He sounded panicked—or disgusted, I couldn't tell. It didn't matter.

"Zachary is already really upset." I tried to sound reasonable.

"You've only known Zachary for a few weeks. You have no idea how much he's been through."

"I know, but—"

"My mom used to get blind stinking drunk and wake

him up in the middle of the night so she could cry on his shoulder."

"Marcus—"

"You have no idea what life was like with her."

"Maybe your mom is getting better."

"Yeah, right."

"You still have Mabel!" I glanced over at Grandpa again. He had looked up from the sink and was listening to the conversation. He turned away when our eyes met, but I could tell his ears were trained on me. I moved across the room and said very softly, "I've known Mabel my whole life. She's a good person."

"No good person could make my mother."

"That's not fair."

He cut across my words. "Don't expect to see me in Denver," and he hung up.

I fought down successive urges to yell into the phone and run outside in total panic, but Grandpa's eyes were on me. I lay the phone in its cradle.

There had to be something I could do, some way to sort this out. If I called the police, Marcus could be arrested. He was angry and rash, but he didn't deserve to go to jail. Still, he was about to disappear with Zachary, and I was the only person who knew about it. I couldn't just let him go.

I couldn't think with Grandpa watching me, so I started to pull myself up the ladder to the loft. "So how about that boat ride?" Grandpa called from the kitchen.

"I just want to lie down for a while."

"You just got up!"

"Please, Grandpa, I need to be alone."

"Was that Marcus? He say something to upset you?"

"No. He's just . . ." I leaned my head on the ladder. This was too much. "He's just mad at Mabel."

"Everything okay?"

I forced a smile. "Yeah."

"Well, why don't we go fishing?"

"Grandpa, I'm just not feeling well this morning."

"You jumped up eagerly enough to get the phone." He stood up from the table and clapped his hands loudly. "Come on! The day's a-wasting."

"I can't."

He turned his cold eyes on me. "You can."

Not this too. Not now. He knew I was upset and wouldn't give me a break. Why was he always so selfish? So determined and intractable and totally oblivious to anything about me? "You know—Just—Get the hell off my case!" I said.

"What did you say?"

"Leave me alone," I said, slowly and quietly.

He enunciated every word: "You are going with me on the river."

"I am going with you nowhere," I enunciated back.

And we stood on opposite sides of the kitchen, glaring at each other, the glacier of his eyes against the immovable wood of mine. Then his shoulders dropped, and to the floor he muttered, "I expected more from this summer."

"Don't you mean you expected more from me?"

"I thought we could spend more time together."

"When you're not with your wonderful Darla?"

"What?"

"Spending time with me has never been a concern of yours before."

"I've always tried to—"

"Oh, please!" I was suddenly overcome with bloodthirsty anger. "Before this summer you never gave me a thought!"

"That's not true."

"It is true, Grandpa. I was just dead weight to you." I locked my eyes on his and glared. "I didn't climb, so I served no purpose for you!"

"You said you didn't want to climb!"

"That's not the point!"

"What is the point?"

"I wanted to climb when I was ten!"

"You were so small, Annie." He seemed confused, as if I'd pulled all this out of thin alpine air. Just more proof I'd been invisible to him all these years!

"If climbing was so dangerous for me, why wasn't it dangerous for Cody?"

"That kid was a born climber, Annie. You saw him!"

"Admit it! You wanted him to climb! You pushed him."

"Of course I did! It's a part of our family!"

"Until it kills us off!"

"Climbing didn't kill Cody, Annie. An avalanche—"

"What's the difference?" I screamed.

"Sweetheart." He came toward me, put his hands on my shoulders. "What does it matter how he died?"

"It does matter! You just don't want to hear it." My voice was raspy and harsh. I didn't even recognize myself, as if I'd become someone else, someone who yells at people. Through my tears I stared right in Grandpa's sad, twisting face. "You started him climbing when he was just a kid! He thought he was immortal."

"He was more careful than climbers twice his age!"

"Until he had a chance to play hero! He walked right into a trap. He walked right into it!"

"Other lives were at stake, Annie." His blue eyes reddened. "He had no choice."

"He did have a choice, and so did you!" I knew I was going too far, but I didn't care. I was like a boulder rolling down a mountainside as I yelled. "You could have saved him!"

He took half a step back. "You don't know what you're saying."

"You killed him." Every word came out of me like a

bullet. I narrowed my eyes and said it again. "You killed Cody."

I watched him curl under my words. He tried to make himself speak, but his lips only parted and closed. Finally he turned his back on me, slammed out the door, got in his truck and drove away.

I stood there breathing hard, feeling like I'd won. I'd finally gotten the best of Jack McGraw. But in the quiet of the living room, my triumph was hollow.

I felt sick to my stomach.

I lay down on the couch. The sunlight soaked through the quilted curtains in the living room, and the colored squares hurt my eyes. I closed them to shut out the light, but then I only saw Grandpa's shocked face, his ice-chip eyes shattered by the things I'd said to him. Even if what I'd said was the truth, I'd been cruel.

This wasn't me. I never yelled at people. I never exploded. Now I'd done it twice, at Marcus in the canoe, and now at Grandpa. It was as if my emotions were land mines waiting for people to trip them with a careless word. I was starting to scare myself.

I wanted to disappear for a while, go to sleep or something, but with a jolt I realized I still had to figure out what to do about Marcus. He would be leaving any minute. He might already be gone, driving off with Zachary to God knows where. I remembered Zachary sobbing next to me on the couch. I had to do something.

Maybe Marcus hadn't left yet. Maybe I could talk him out of this. I picked up the phone and dialed his number.

Marcus answered after the second ring. "Zachary?"

"What? No, it's Annie!"

"Is Zachary there?" His voice was frantic.

"What?"

He took a deep breath and said very firmly, "Is Zachary there?"

"No! Why would he be?"

"Annie, I need your help."

"I'm not helping you take Zachary."

"Shut up and listen!" His voice was shrill. "I can't find him anywhere."

"Good, then you can't leave."

"Shut up! You don't understand. He's gone, Annie! Zachary's missing!"

26

Marcus was driving way too fast. A huge cloud of dust rose behind the car, stirred up by the tires on the loose-dirt roads. I kept reminding him to slow down or we could miss Zachary somewhere, but panic made his foot heavy on the gas pedal. We'd checked Mabel's back-yard and the forest surrounding it; we'd called everyone we knew within walking distance of Mabel's house. I'd even taken Marcus to the Tepee Tree, sure Zachary would have gone there, but there was no sign of him.

"How long has it been since you last saw him?" I asked.

"I don't know. Five hours?" He glanced at his wrist, though there was no watch there, then hit the steering wheel with the heel of his hand. "I was busy packing our bags."

"Did he say anything?"

"No! I told you! He just disappeared."

"How could he just disappear?"

He slowed down as we passed a family on the side of the road. There was a dark-haired little boy with them, but it wasn't Zachary. "I don't know."

"Do you think he meant to disappear?"

"Maybe."

"Why?"

He glanced at me, seeming to mull his words, then finally admitted, "He was mad. Okay? He didn't want to go and he was mad at me."

"So he probably meant to disappear, then, right?"

He shrugged.

"Does he have his jacket with him?" Marcus didn't respond. "Marcus! Does he have warm clothes?"

"Probably not, Annie. It's summer."

It made no difference. A lot of people get hypothermia in the summer because the heat of the day is deceptive. Thin mountain air cools quickly with sundown, and we only had another few hours of sunlight left. If we didn't find him soon, Zachary would probably be spending the night outside.

"Marcus, we should call Search and Rescue."

"This isn't like him." He accelerated, scanning the road frantically.

"We need more people to help."

"He's afraid of the dark. He'll show up before then."

"Not if he's lost! Turn around and get us to a ranger station, now!"

Reluctantly, he slowed the car down and stopped by the side of the road. "This is my fault," he muttered. "He didn't want to leave tonight, but I wouldn't listen."

"We have to go now, Marcus." I didn't feel like sympathizing. He wouldn't give Mabel a chance, he wouldn't listen to me, and now Zachary was missing in a million acres of forest. "Come on. Drive."

"Okay. Yes. You're right." He turned the car around.

We found a ranger station near one of the lakes, tucked into a cubbyhole log cabin. Marcus parked and bounded up the steps with one long-legged leap. He pushed his way past several people who were waiting in line at the counter and burst out at the ranger, "My little brother is missing!"

The ranger looked at him sternly. "How old is he?"

"He's seven."

The ranger beckoned another, whose paunch hung over his belt buckle like a sack of grain. The man led Marcus into a room in the back of the cabin.

I stayed behind to call Mabel and see if Zachary had shown up there. She picked up on the first ring. "Hello?"

"Mabel—"

"Annie? I've been trying to call you! Are the boys with you?"

"Marcus is with me."

Her voice took on a wary cast. "Where's Zachary?"

"We don't know." I heard her take a deep breath as I did the same. "We've been looking for him all day, Mabel."

"Oh God." Her voice crumbled. "Where are you?"

"We're at a ranger station. We're just letting Search and Rescue know, then we'll be right home."

"Search and Rescue?"

I listened to her breathing quicken. I didn't want to scare her, but it seemed more important we get all the help we could. "He might be lost in the woods, Mabel, and it's getting dark soon."

"I'll call around to the neighbors," she said, and hung up.

I went into the back office to find Marcus pacing the floor. The ranger was on a wireless giving Zachary's physical description in a nasal drone. "About forty-five pounds . . . three feet eight inches, dark brown hair and eyes, seven years old, last seen north of the Colter Bay area . . ." He looked over at Marcus apprehensively before he continued. "Recommend Snake River boat patrol . . . recommend public announcement."

Then we were back in the car, leading the ranger in

his pickup to Mabel's cabin. She was waiting on the porch, shifting from foot to foot. When Marcus got out of the car she lunged, giving him a desperate hug. "Why didn't you call me sooner?"

She turned to me, smoothing my hair out of my face. "Where's your grandfather?"

I shook my head, but then it struck me that he must be at Darla's. Mabel rushed in to call.

High, scattered clouds touched by the colors of roses were spreading over the tops of the trees. The beauty was ominous. I imagined the dusk bearing down on Zachary with each deepening hue, the dark night folding itself around him. Wherever he was, he was probably scared.

Neighbors began to arrive in pickups, vans, old convertibles. A dozen mill workers Marcus had called cascaded off the back of an ancient flatbed truck, carrying lanterns and coffee thermoses. Six rangers arrived in a green van and started splitting everyone into groups. They passed out dozens of radios. When they ran out of radios, they handed out whistles, barking directions like drill sergeants. Ned from Nora's Fish Creek Inn tooled up in his pickup, with Nora in the passenger's seat. Some of the searchers helped her unload the huge coffee machine that she had brought from the restaurant, and she took it into the kitchen, along with hundreds of plastic cups and pounds of coffee, yelling at the men to stay out of the house.

As quickly as they came, they fanned out, their flashlights waving haphazardly among the tree trunks, their voices robust, calling Zachary's name. Mabel stood on the porch shivering, her big arms tight around Marcus's shoulders. His face was white as he stared into the darkness.

Mabel patted his head gently. "It's time we call your mother, and then you can go look too."

I started to follow them inside when I heard my name called. Joseph sprinted up to me. "Where is everyone?"

"They all went to look for Zachary."

He threw his hands up. "They'll destroy his trail! I won't be able to track him." He ran inside, shouting questions at Marcus, then burst back out and walked around and around the cabin in a widening circle, his lantern and bright eyes trained on the ground.

Grandpa jogged up with Darla. "Who saw him last?" he asked quietly, his gaze not quite meeting mine.

"Marcus," I mumbled, and Grandpa was gone, inside the cabin. I sat down on the porch steps and buried my face in my hands. Darla stood over me, her thumbs hooked in her belt loops. "Bloody awful mess."

I nodded.

She smiled uncomfortably at me, then went up the stairs and into the house. Grandpa must have told her about our fight and the things I said.

I heard the phone ring inside and rushed in to see if it was news of Zachary. Mabel was saying, "Okay. Drive careful. We'll see you then." Hanging up, she turned to Marcus. "She's leaving right away. She'll be here by tomorrow morning."

Marcus started pacing. "I can't wait anymore. I'm going to look for him." He grabbed a flashlight off the table and ran out. Mabel handed me a canteen and said, "You go with him. He doesn't know his way around."

I nodded, eager for something to do. Outside, the game warden handed us two whistles on shoestrings and told us to blow on them when we found Zachary. *When* we found him.

We took a trail that led away from the river, calling Zachary's name, but our voices were dispersed by the rustling wind. I heard Grandpa's husky voice moving down south of us and was startled at how quickly his call faded away. How could we find Zachary in darkness like this? He was a tiny little boy in a million acres of dense forest. I remembered the day in Yellowstone when he'd wandered off, right to the edge of a hot pool. How could he survive out here? I swallowed hard and tried not to think about all the things that could happen to him. Hypothermia. Dehydration. He could get weak and pass out in a thicket somewhere.

Or a bear could find him.

Marcus and I pushed into the darkness.

Midnight, one, two, three . . . As each hour passed, Marcus grew more frantic. There were times I wanted to yell at him, blame him for what happened, but I knew that wouldn't help Zachary. We weaved back and forth, going down this trail for an hour, looping back on another trail for an hour, doing it again. My ankles were swollen. Every joint creaked like a rusty hinge. I stumbled, scraping my knees so many times that I had to let the blood trail down my shins and into my socks. Marcus's face was matted with layers of trail dust and sweat, making it look like an eerie road map in the dim glow of our flashlights.

I looked at my watch. It was four in the morning. "We're out of water," I said for the third time. "We've got to go back for a little while, Marcus."

"I can't leave him." He kept walking ahead of me, wiping his runny nose on his sleeve.

"Marcus, there might be news. We should go back."

He stopped, looked through the woods, scanning every tree, turning his lantern on every movement before he finally let his head droop and followed me back to the cabin. If he'd only listened to me instead of insisting on his idiotic plan, we wouldn't be looking for

Zachary out here. But it didn't seem right to think about that now. After hours and hours of following him around while he frantically searched for his little brother, it was clear that even if he'd acted like a jerk, he really did love Zachary.

After another hour of picking our way through dark forest trails, we stumbled into the cabin. We stepped over about a dozen snoring men on the floor. Darla was sleeping in Mabel's armchair.

We found Mabel sitting at her kitchen table, fidgeting over a cup of coffee. She popped right up. "Any word?"

Marcus shook his head despairingly.

She sighed, gave me her chair, and silently made us eggs and toast. After we'd eaten, she sternly sent us off to bed for a few hours' sleep. With a dry, vulnerable voice, Marcus asked her to wake him up if there was any news. We collapsed on the only empty bed in the house, and he put his arms around me, his head on my shoulder. I was so exhausted I didn't even register that we were in bed together. I took off my unused whistle and then his, and set them on the bedside table. I patted his head, picking twigs out of his thick hair, until finally the light of dawn was hidden by my leaden eyelids, and I fell asleep.

27

I woke up alone. There were excited voices in the kitchen, and I quickly rubbed the sleep from my eyes and rushed down to see if there was any news.

Penny was downstairs, sitting at the kitchen table, smoking a cigarette, her voice husky. "I don't see how you could even think of doing such a thing, Marcus. How could either of you?" She flashed a look of anger at Mabel, who stood leaning on the refrigerator, fingering the hem of a faded blue-striped curtain.

Marcus was shaking with fury. "Neither of you seemed to care how Zachary felt about any of this—"

Mabel roared, "Nothing I did was an easy decision, Marcus."

Penny slammed her fist on the table. "Shut up! Both of you!"

Mabel noticed me and closed her eyes in humiliation. Penny looked at me blankly. I retreated to the living room.

Darla was sitting on a chair sipping at a mug. Her eyes were half closed from lack of sleep. When I came in she handed me her coffee. "Take it. I've had far too much." She leaned back on the couch, her head on the cushions. "The weather forecast calls for rain, Anna. And it might snow higher up. We must find him soon." I glanced out the window and saw dark clouds hanging over the valley.

Zachary wouldn't survive a snowy night.

The voices from the kitchen screeched shrilly through the walls. Darla and I cringed. "A terrible shame." She shook her head. "They need each other now."

I sipped at my coffee irritably. "They need a referee."

She waved away my words. "I learned the hard way how important family is. It's more important than anything else, even when our lives with them are unhappy."

"It's not that simple."

"Actually, it is," she said, her gray eyes fixed on me. "And it's something you would do well to learn."

"Okay." I was too exhausted and anxious to be polite. "I'll get right on it."

"I won't apologize for Jack, Anna. He's not perfect. But I'm convinced his greatest flaw is how he underestimates himself."

"I don't see it that way."

"That's just how he replied when I said that to him yesterday!" She scoffed. "You're just like him, you know that?"

"We're nothing alike."

"You are both shy, gruff, and stubborn. Reaching out to you both is like trying to pet a snapping turtle! If you don't bite, you go right into your shell and won't come out for anything!"

I paused. She'd come awfully close to describing the armadillo defense.

"You know," she continued in utter exasperation, "in his way he has tried to reach out to you, and you shut him down every time." She looked at me gravely. I realized I'd said almost exactly the same thing to Zachary only a couple days before when I told him to stop shutting me out. "We can't choose our families. We do choose our behavior. And Anna, quite frankly, you have chosen badly."

"You don't know anything about it," I snapped.

Her voice rose in a caw. "Poppycock! I know grief and I know Jack McGraw! You hurt your grandfather deeply yesterday, Anna. He's been out there looking for that little boy for fourteen hours without a break. He's punishing himself like this because he's trying to make up for not being able to save Cody. Can't you see how much pain he's in over Cody's death? And how silently he's trying to bear it to protect you? Can't you see that's an act of love, even if he's wrong to do it?"

"He's protecting himself." I was so tired I could only speak the truth about how I felt, even before I knew what the truth was. "He never cared about me when he had Cody. Now that I'm the only grandkid, he needs me."

"Poppycock again, Anna."

"He never talks to me."

"Darling, *you* never talk to *him*! It might seem ludicrous to you, but he thinks you never liked him! And Cody kept him busy, dear, with climbing lessons. He was a wonderful boy, but it sounds to me like he did everything he could to stay in the spotlight." She put her hand on mine. I pulled mine away. Gently she said, "Jack has always loved you. He admires you. Your intelligence, your spirit. He thinks you're wonderful."

Tears threatened. "He doesn't."

"He *does*. He *does*, Anna." She put her hand on mine again and this time I didn't have the strength to pull away. Carefully, she said, "I think the person who doesn't like you is *you*, dear."

I sat perfectly still. I couldn't look at her.

We heard Mabel burst into tears, and Marcus's mom yelling even more.

I couldn't stand to hear their fighting. I couldn't stand to sit there. I couldn't stand to be near Darla because of what else she might say. I slipped my hand from under hers. "I have to go."

She nodded.

I grabbed a fresh canteen from where it hung on the wall and went out the door. My knees were sore and stiff with scabs that popped open as I stumbled down the porch steps. Troops of exhausted men swarmed around the cabin, their eyes hanging heavy in their faces. "Still no sign," one of them said to me. I chose a trail and followed it away from the cabin, too tired to even call Zachary's name.

Still no sign, still no sign. I repeated the words in time with my footsteps. I didn't pay attention to where I was going. What would be the point? I just kept heading uphill, further and further, my feet and legs numb, my eyes heavy, my jaw clamped shut.

I ran into some searchers heading back on the trail toward the cabin. They shook their heads. "Still no sign."

I broke off the trail and bushwhacked uphill. Branches snapped against my face. I wiped a bead of blood from my chin. I didn't care that I was bleeding.

Still no sign.

I set my sights on the southern peak of the Tetons so I wouldn't lose my bearings. I scanned the trees for Zachary's little pale face, his purple satchel, his green jacket. "Zachary, where are you?" I had said it aloud, softly, before I realized I'd spoken at all. My voice sounded strange to me, hoarse, barely audible. The voice of a stranger.

Still no sign.

We had to get to Zachary soon. With no food or

shelter, he wouldn't last another night. Storm clouds were already cutting off the sun, casting quick-moving shadows over the forest. *Zachary, hang on, kid. Please. Don't do this to me. I can't go through this again.*

The incline of the ground got steeper. I was on the slope of the Tetons, probably farther than Zachary would have walked by himself, but I couldn't turn back to the cabin. Waiting felt like a trap closing around me. At least in the forest, searching alone, far from ticking clocks, I could push away the thought that if we didn't find him soon, our search would be for a body.

A body we'll never find. A frozen corpse in the mountains—

I couldn't let myself think like that. I sped up, feeding my steps with the pain in my legs, making myself numb to it. I saw a straight line uphill and forced my body into the rhythm of a hike, feeling each footstep in my hips, my back, and the throbbing in my head.

The forest was dense here. Dead and dying trees lay across my path, rotting into a rust-colored dust, sticking up sharp branches that caught my clothes. Thickets of dried-out bushes twined in my path but to save time, I fought my way through, scratching my face on the hard twigs.

I wanted to be scratched. I deserved to be scratched. For wanting Marcus so much I ignored his stupid plan. For not telling Mabel about it. For being weak and little and cowardly. For not being able to climb. Afraid of heights. For sleeping all day when Mom had to go to work. For screaming at Grandpa. For being alive when Cody wasn't. For everything, everything. For losing him.

I burst through a net of branches only to find twice as many ahead of me. I tore through those, ripping my T-shirt on them, pricking my arms. My face stung as though each branch were laced with venom. The further I went, the thicker my trap, until the bushes held me in a constrictive embrace, rubbing my ribs, refusing to yield no matter how hard I leaned against them. I grunted like my grandfather, my teeth gnashing, my sweat and blood running in streams over my face. I stood there, defeated, panting, peering through the lattice for a way out. I was exhausted. More exhausted than I had ever been. My head was light, my vision bleary. I felt my mind bending under the pressure.

And I recognized this place. Dream forest.

Dimly the trees hung in a black curtain around me. The smell of the woods unraveled into a thousand messages in the breeze. I smelled her again, as on that first morning on the riverbank, the thick scent of her food and her waste, her heavy breath and the soil in her coat.

I am not alone. I have never been alone. I am never alone.

I saw her. My heart thumped wildly and I had to gulp air or faint. She was five yards away, looking at me over her haunches. She lifted her snout to the breeze, caught my scent, then studied me, her tawny, pinpoint eyes focused precisely on mine. She opened her mouth, bared her teeth. She was panting now, grunting and panting through an awful grin. I sank to my knees, trembling. I could feel how soft my skin would be to her, how tender, how easily torn by those teeth.

She turned away from me, uninterested, to lick something between her paws. It made a thin, papery sound.

A candy bar wrapper. She was licking a candy bar wrapper.

I scanned the forest floor and saw more of them strewn among the wildflower petals and mildewed leaves.

He is here.

I crawled through the branches as slowly and quietly as I could, watching her. She looked at me again, then lumbered uphill to another wrapper. I forced myself to breathe more slowly and followed.

She worked her way up the hill, tolerating me as she ambled to the next wrapper, and the next. I was shaking, faint, terrified that she would change her mind about me and bare her teeth. But she showed no interest at all. She was on the trail of more chocolate, and I was sure, down to my bones, that these wrappers had been the contents of Zachary's satchel. Every step she took brought us closer to him.

She headed directly uphill until the forest eased into a worn path on the ridge of the mountain. The tremor of a waterfall murmured through the air, and I recognized this place.

As she walked along the edge of the cliff, I listened to the falls in their perennial exchange: air to river to ocean to air, forever. The grizzly lifted her snout to the mist, and I lifted my face. Droplets kissed me each individually, many at once.

The bear grunted. *He needs you.*

I can't reach him.

You have to find him.

I'm so alone without him.

You are never alone.

Help me find him. I want him back.

You always have him. He needs you now.

Where is he? Tell me where.

And she was nearer, nearer still, so near now I felt her warm breath on my face. And I was so tired, so tired I could have slept on my feet, and I wanted to. And she swayed to the rhythm of falling water, rainwater, cascades and dew, and I swayed with her, north to south, north and north, further and further. The rumble of the falls approached me.

The empty space behind me opened to receive my body.

I stopped myself.

He needs you.

Don't ask me this.

She backed away from me, sauntered to some bushes and roughly dragged a heavy shape from underneath. She poked her muzzle into it, turned it over. I heard fabric ripping. I didn't want to look but I had to look, for him, I had to know.

Zachary's satchel.

She looked at me, her brown eyes searching my face. Swiftly, violently, she took the sack in her jaws and flung it into the canyon.

The bear walked closer to the edge, sniffed the air, looked at me askance. And walked away. Down the hill.

And I was alone.

28

"Zachary! Where are you? Zachary! Answer me!" I screamed over and over, into the rumble of the falls, screaming, screaming, "Zachary," against the wind and the water, "Zachary," into the endless sky and the bottomless chasm, "Zachary" until my voice broke.

And I was on my knees, out of breath, ready to weep.

Then I heard it. A human voice woven like spider's silk into the web of the falls. "Help!" it called from below. Far below.

"Zachary?"

"Annie?"

"Where are you?" I called into the plummet, weeping in relief.

"Down here!"

I tried to approach the edge, but I couldn't stand to get any closer. "Where?"

"Below you. Get me out of here!"

I turned my back on the canyon and screamed into the forest: "I need help! Can anyone hear me? Help!" I screamed as loudly as I could, then waited for what seemed forever.

There was no answer except for the distant sound of Zachary crying.

Why did I leave my whistle at Mabel's house? Even if I'd had it, I doubted any of the searchers were within earshot. Who would ever guess that Zachary had gone this far?

He's down there. He's down there and I can't get to him. Zachary is alive and I can't help him because I can't go down there. I can't.

"Can you climb up, Zachary?"

"I don't know!" His voice splintered like green wood. He was at his breaking point.

"Take a deep breath and look up. How far down are you?"

"The rock is rounded. I can't see."

"Try pulling yourself up. Can you do that?"

"I tried before, Annie! It's too smooth!"

"Try again, Zachary. Try climbing toward my voice."

"I don't want to."

"Did you climb down there?"

"Yes."

"Then you can climb up. Try."

I stood near the ledge, drumming my foot nervously on the rock as I waited for him, my whole body filled with electric fear. "How's it going?"

"I think I'm doing it."

"You're climbing?"

"Yes!" he yelled.

What if he falls? "Zachary? Wait a second."

"What?" he screamed, furious.

"Don't climb up."

"Don't?"

"I'm going for help." *Stupid. I should have thought of this before.*

"Annie! Don't go!"

"I'll be back. We need ropes. We can do this safer."

"Don't go!"

"Climb back down to the ledge, Zachary, and wait for me there."

"Climb back *down*?"

"Yes, Zachary. Just climb back down." There was no answer. "Zachary?" Still no answer. "Zachary!"

"Shut up!"

"Are you back on the ledge?"

"No!" He was crying. "I can't move!"

"Yes you can, Zachary."

"I can't move my arms."

"Why?"

"I don't know!" He was nearly hysterical.

"Zachary, take deep breaths. Calm down."

"I can't. I'm scared."

"Deep breaths, deep breaths."

I waited for a minute, then asked, "Are you calm now?"

"I guess," he snuffled.

"Okay, now can you move?"

"No!" He started to panic again. "Annie, you have to help me!"

"I'll get help, Zachary."

"I can't wait that long!"

"Climb down to the ledge!"

"I can't move you—*Stupid!*" Now he was hysterical.

"Okay. Just don't panic, okay?" I ran my fingers through my hair to make my hands stop shaking. They shook more. I knew what I had to do; there was no other way. *Get it together, Annie, just pull yourself together,* I said over and over as I got on my belly and forced myself to hang my head over the lip of the rock.

The floor of the canyon fell away like the false bottom of a trick box. I spread my fingers on the rock underneath me and clung to it as I felt myself tipping. My head swam and I threw up a little. Vomit trickled down the rock. I forced my eyes to follow the sound of Zachary's crying until I saw a tiny brown shape, the top of his shaggy head, about thirty feet down, peeking over a swell in the smooth rock. I yelled, "Try one more time, Zachary. Please?"

I saw him cast his hand around, shifting his weight. He leaned his forehead on the rock, beyond his strength.

There was no other way. I had to get to him now. "Stay there!" I yelled. "I'm coming for you!"

I got up and sprinted along the edge, stopping every few yards to look down for a route. Soon I was almost to the end of the trail, so near the falls that I felt their thunder through the soles of my shoes. Finally the sheer rock face broke into boulders I could shimmy down. I squeezed into the spaces between the rocks, jamming my toes into cracks and bracing myself on flat palms as I descended into the canyon. It was at least a two-hundred-foot drop. I tried to keep my vision focused just ahead of me, but I could feel the hard rocks below pulling at my body. I forced myself to focus on the wall as I worked my way from foothold to foothold. The rock was slippery wet, and I had to go slowly, but I couldn't go too slowly. Every pause put Zachary in greater danger.

He was somewhere to my left, about sixty feet, so I moved in that direction, picking my way through rocks, then a slope of pebbles, until I came to the place where the rock was clean and smooth.

I looked, but I couldn't see Zachary. He was hidden by the curve of the cliff.

To my left was a horizontal crack in the rock wall that extended in Zachary's direction. I eased over to it and kicked my toes into the fissure before I could look down.

Nothing but air for two hundred feet.

The bottom of everything fell away and I remembered where I was.

I froze.

I can't do this.

I closed my eyes and concentrated on calming myself. I pictured Cody, clinging to a wall like this one, his elbows at right angles, all his weight on his feet, his body perfectly straight. He only ever moved one limb at a time, first one arm, then the other, then one leg, then the other, slowly, methodically, until he'd reached the top. That's what it was. That's what climbing was.

I swallowed saliva until my nausea went away. I stared at the rock in front of me until my balance was assured. And then I started moving toward Zachary.

I sidled along the wall, focusing on footholds and handholds, my toes wedged into the crack in the rock.

I remembered what Cody had told me. *Climbing is like a devotion.*

I finally understood. There was no room for my fear. Everything depended on my hands and feet and their connection to the earth. Nothing else.

And I knew I could climb because I *was* climbing.

I rounded the bend in the rock to see Zachary below and still to my left. He was about twenty feet above a narrow ledge. His face was turned up toward me, his cheek pressed against the cold rock. His arms were shaking, his lips quaked with fear, but his eyes were angry. He hadn't given up yet.

I shimmied along the crack until it ended within a few yards of him. He watched my progress, hopeful. I had to yell over the falls. "I see the ledge, Zachary. We'll go there." Feeling around with my toes for jagged holds, I edged my way down to him until I was right next to him. Lightly, I touched his arm with my elbow. He tried to say something, but his lip shook and he bit it until it was white.

"Can you see the ledge?"

Barely, he shook his head, whimpering. "I was there all night."

"Well, we can't stay here, can we?"

Again, he shook his head. The movement dislodged his right hand and he screamed. I grabbed his wrist and forced it back into his handhold. "My arms hurt."

"We have to climb down."

"I can't move." His whole body was shaking with fatigue.

"Try."

"I can't. I've been here too long."

I believed him. My own hands and arms were already burning. I had to move soon or my muscles would seize up. We had to get out of here or we both might die.

"Zachary, if I move right next to you, can you put your arms around my shoulders like a piggyback ride?"

"I don't know." His voice was shaking like the rest of him.

"Zachary! You have three choices. You can climb down yourself, you can get on my back, or you can fall. Which is it?"

"Piggyback."

I wasn't sure I could support both his weight and my own, but I didn't see another way. "Okay. First put your right arm on my shoulder nearest you."

Fumbling, he did as I said. I felt the strain of the added weight in my back. I tried to get a little closer to him by shifting farther to my left. He groped, whimpering, terrified that I was going to push him off.

"Just see if you can wrap your right leg around my waist."

"I can't." His fingernails were digging into my shoulder.

"You have to, Zachary."

He started to cry. I moved a little closer to him so that our torsos touched. He was so small. He must be really light. For a moment all my fear left and I knew I could carry him to the ledge. "Zachary, you've gotten on Marcus for piggyback rides before, right?"

He nodded, sniffling.

"You're going to have to pretend that this is one of those times. So on the count of three, we're going to do this. Okay?"

He nodded again.

"Ready? One . . ."

His right arm slid over onto my right shoulder.

"Two . . ."

He wriggled his toe, grinding pebbles out of the rock wall to fall hundreds of feet.

"Three!"

He swung his leg around, flailing at my waist like a rag doll. He screamed, wildly out of control. Fighting down panic, I kicked further into my foothold and grabbed his skinny thigh with my right hand. His swinging stopped and I pulled him up as high as I could so that he could wrap his legs around my waist.

My calves felt like they would split, but we were steady. I tried to sound calm as I said, "I've got you. You've got to let go of the rock with your other hand."

"You won't drop me?"

Firmly, I said, "No."

We looked at each other, our faces stony, our breath suddenly steady. In his dirty, scratched face, I saw the eyes of a grizzly cub, solid and tender, looking back at me. His mouth tightened, his jaw set, and he said, "Okay. Count to three." I forced my aching fingers into a stronger hold, "One, two, three."

He whipped his other hand around my neck and clung to me. I groaned under his weight. He was heavier than he looked.

We didn't have much time.

I dropped my left foot down, feeling for a hold, then my right, then my left. Sweat poured into my eyes. My face swelled from the pressure of Zachary's grip around my neck. I could only peer down with my peripheral vision, unable to risk leaning out to look for the ledge.

"Zachary, can you see the ledge?"

"No. You're in the way."

I groped with my left foot to find only empty space. I inched further down and again felt for it, but found nothing. Nothing. My shoulders seared, my fingers were sweaty, and my body was in a spasm of fatigue. I had to find the ledge right away.

"Zachary, you have to look for it."

His weight shifted, pulling us away from the wall.

"Don't lean out! Don't lean out!" I was shrieking.

"The ledge disappeared! I can't see it!" He held my neck hard, scooting his legs further up my body. The pain in my shoulders was unbearable, so I started down again, biting my lip hard to keep from crying. With my left foot I groped for a hold, and again found nothing but sheer rock. I tried with my right foot, whimpering in despair. Nothing.

Muscles seized. My body rebelled. My fingers were slipping.

"Oh God," I heard myself say.

Two screams tore into the sky as we fell like stones from the wall.

29

"My butt hurts."

"Well, you landed on it pretty hard."

"Can I have more water?"

I handed him my canteen and he took a long drink. He was very dehydrated.

When I had felt my grip loosen from the wall, I was sure Zachary and I were dead, but the entire time we had been looking for the ledge, it had been directly below us. We landed hard, and I twisted my ankle badly, but otherwise both of us were fine.

For the moment.

"Go easy on it, Zachary. We don't know how long we'll be stuck up here."

I pushed on my sore muscles with my fingertips, trying to hide my fear. There were only about five more hours of daylight left, and the mist from the falls was drenching our clothes. We were both shivering from fatigue and cold, and storm clouds were hanging low and threatening. It would be a cold night, much colder than the last. A night outside with no room to move around would mean hypothermia, and I doubted we could survive the exposure. I had to think of a way to let someone know we were here.

"Keep looking for people, Zachary. It's the middle of tourist season. There has to be someone out and about." He leaned forward and squinted hard across the canyon to the rock wall on the other side of the falls. He was absolutely filthy, his face scratched and oozing blood in places. There were dark circles under his eyes, but he seemed much calmer now.

"Zachary, you still haven't told me how you ended up here."

"It was dark last night." His eyebrows were cinched angrily over his big brown eyes. He sniffed. "I went into the trees to get out of the wind, and there was a monster."

"Monsters don't exist."

"Yes they do," he said with conviction. "I ran away from it. I couldn't see where I was going, and I slid off the edge."

My jaw dropped. "You fell from the cliff onto this ledge? That's got to be at least fifty feet!"

He shook his head. "I slid for a little way on the rounded part, and then I caught myself. I couldn't go up because of the monster, so I kept climbing down until I hit the ledge. I didn't know how high up I was until morning."

"What did the monster look like?"

"Big and round, and it grunted."

I smiled. "That wasn't a monster, Zach. It was a bear."

His eyes widened. "Like your bear?"

"I think so."

His gaze shifted into the canyon as he pondered this.

"Zachary, why did you run away? Marcus has been going crazy, and Mabel too."

He shrugged.

"No shrugging! I just saved your life. I think I deserve an explanation."

"I didn't want to run away with Marcus, but he was going to make me." Angrily, he hit his palm on the rock. "I left because I was mad."

"That's the only reason?"

"I wanted to make him worry. I don't like all the fighting. Mom and Marcus always fought about me. Now Mabel is fighting with them. And Marcus was going to make me go away with him, but I didn't want to. It isn't fair. Everybody is always making me do things I don't want to do." He stuck out his bottom lip far enough for a bird to land on it.

"So you ran away?"

"I just wanted to hide so Marcus couldn't leave. I wanted to find that tree where we were that day, but I couldn't find it. And when night came I couldn't find my way back."

"We thought you were trying to run away."

"I left so I wouldn't *have* to run away with *Marcus*. He's a big dummy."

I rubbed his back. "You're right. He is a big dummy."

He gazed into the canyon for a few minutes, but then his brow wrinkled in confusion. "How did you find me?"

"A monster showed me where you were." We looked in each other's eyes.

"Monsters can be good," he said.

"Yes."

Suddenly Zachary bolted upright, kicking rocks over the edge. "There are some people!"

"Where?"

He pointed across the canyon. I squinted at the rock wall opposite us. "I don't see anything."

He sighed, frustrated. "They're right there! Climbing on the rocks."

I peered across. There were two people so far away

they weren't even a centimeter tall. One of them was climbing up the cliff face. His companion was below, holding on to his climbing rope for him, watching his progress.

"Hey!" we screamed, our voices lost in the tumble of the falls.

They didn't even look up. I tried throwing rocks at them, but they plummeted pitifully into the canyon.

Zachary picked up the canteen, nearly dropping it over the edge. "Be careful!" I yelled. "That's all we've got." I tried to take it away from him, but he jerked it out of my hands.

"It's shiny. Maybe they'll see its reflection."

I watched as he angled the shiny metal canteen to reflect the sun's rays at the climbers, but the clouds were too thick for a bright beam.

"Keep it up, Zachary. Maybe the clouds will break." I stood up, careful not to jostle my ankle, and waved my arms to try to catch their eye. I hated myself for forgetting my whistle at Mabel's. I screamed until my voice cracked, but they just kept practicing their belay.

Zachary started crying and put the canteen down. Between his sniffles he said, "It was cold last night, Annie. I couldn't feel my hands."

The skin on his fingers was white and soft-looking, mildly frostbitten. I sat down again and patted his shoulder. "Tonight you'll sleep in your grandma's house, Zachary." I only half believed it myself, and I knew he could hear the doubt in my voice. Then I remembered the perfect thing to cheer him up. "Hey! Guess who's here."

"Who?" he whined, wiping his nose on his sleeve.

"Your mom! She was so worried about you that she drove here last night. She's waiting for you at Mabel's."

He brightened. "Really? Mom's here?"

"Yeah, so you keep reflecting the sun at those people and we'll get home to see her tonight."

He sat up with the canteen pointed at the men. Tears still wet his face, but he was determined to be found.

I cupped my hands around my mouth and yelled as loudly as I could, but my voice was so tired that I could barely make more than a croak. Zachary yelled too, until we both ran out of breath. We sat there panting, staring hard at the climbers, trying to send them messages by telepathy.

In the quiet, something caught my ear as faint as a whisper. My name? It was so distant and I was so tired that I didn't trust my own ears. I turned to Zachary. "Did you hear that?"

Zachary knit his brows, listening to the wind, his head cocked. Again came the faint, ghostly call. "*Annie . . .*"

His brows lifted. "Yes. I hear it! We're here!" he screamed.

Again came the call, and this time we both yelled, "Here! We're here!" Suddenly I was even more scared. What if they didn't hear us, or the echo of the canyon sent them looking in a different direction? I screamed again, "Here! Here!" I clapped my hands wildly and the sound reverberated off the rock walls around us. I paused to listen.

Silence. We both sat there, trembling, straining to listen. Zachary squeezed my arm. I could feel the tremor of his fear in his fingers. Then suddenly the voice was above us. "Annie?" It was Grandpa. Grandpa had found us.

I croaked, "Down here! Grandpa! We're here!" My voice was wavering and I realized I was crying. I'd never been so relieved in my life.

"Where are you?" His voice was right above us.

Zachary called, "Down here on a ledge." Zachary's hand clamped harder on my arm as he yelled, "Below you!"

A pause, then, "Who's that?"

"It's me, Zachary! Annie, too, but a frog is in her throat."

"How the—" I heard him blow on his rescue whistle. "Can you climb up?"

"Hell no," I called irritably.

"There were some climbers a quarter mile back. I'll go borrow their rope. Don't move."

"Don't worry."

I gave Zachary a hug and leaned against the rock. The pain in my back and shoulders lessened, and I realized I had been tensing them the whole time. Now that we'd been found, I realized how scared I'd been that we wouldn't make it back. Everything was going to be okay.

It took Grandpa only about fifteen minutes before he was back and lowering himself down the cliff wearing a nylon climbing harness. He dropped onto the ledge, crowding Zachary and me against the wall. I had never been so glad to see anyone. He put his hand on my shoulder and looked into my eyes. "You okay?"

"Yeah." I nodded, though my ankle was killing me.

"You're all bloody." He dabbed a bandanna on my forehead, and I remembered I'd scratched myself in the bracken.

"It doesn't hurt."

He looked at me quizzically. "Odd time to take up climbing."

"It wasn't by choice."

He knelt down and looked Zachary over carefully. He examined his hands, turning them over gently. "You'll be fine." He mussed his hair as he stood up again, saying, "You caused a stir."

"I didn't mean to," Zachary said, shamefaced.

"Glad to see you in one piece." Grandpa took a deep breath and looked at the sky. His face was streaked with trail dust, and sweat stains had seeped low on his plaid shirt. The sleepless night of wandering trails made him look about ten years older. He was stiff and sluggish as he wriggled out of the climbing harness and helped Zachary put it on. Zachary rested his tiny hand on Grandpa's massive shoulder, letting himself be tugged and maneuvered until finally he was strapped in tight. Grandpa knelt down and looked him square in the eye. "Now listen to me. A couple of guys'll pull you up. They only have one harness, so this is the safest way. Keep your feet to the rock and walk up. Don't bounce, and don't swing, or you could get bruised awful bad. Got it?"

Zachary nodded, swallowing hard. Grandpa called up, "Okay. Pull him up slow."

Slowly the rope inched up, and Zachary scaled the wall just as Grandpa had said. As he watched him go, Grandpa gave one shake of the head. "Natural." Then he turned to me. Alone again, our silence became uncomfortable, as always. Finally he said, "Overcome your fear of heights?"

"More scared than ever, actually."

"Damn lucky I noticed your tracks. Never would've come up here."

"How did you know the tracks were mine?"

"Size five. Pigeon-toed. Right foot scrapes to the right. Been that way ever since you were little."

Only Grandpa would know that about me. I looked at him. He took a deep breath of the air—air scoured clean by the waterfall. Head high, chest out, he scanned the canyon below with his boreal eyes. Perched on a ledge too small for a big dog to turn on, he was completely at home. He was my grandfather, and he knew my shoe size and the pattern of my step.

"Why were you looking for me, Grandpa?"

"Hungry. Thought you might have a sandwich." He glanced at me sideways, then added, "And I was worried. I just wanted to, you know . . . check on you."

"I know." I wanted to say I was sorry about our fight, but I couldn't think of a way to start, so I just stood next to him, watching the falls.

"You're right, you know," Grandpa finally said.

"About what?"

"About Cody. I had a bad feeling about that expedition. Bad peak for his first trip down there. I encouraged him anyway." His eyes reddened as he lowered his chin toward the gap at our feet. He seemed to shrink six inches under an unbearable weight.

Standing next to him on that rock ledge, I saw how much older he'd become, how broken he was from Cody's death. And I understood. What Darla had said was true. We were alike.

The light was gray as the sun filtered through the storm clouds and plunged into the mist at the foot of the falls. No wonder Cody had climbed—to see views like this. "Grandpa, I was wrong," I said. I had to force out every word, but I knew I couldn't let what I'd said fester any longer. I was beginning to see that it wasn't just hurting him; it was hurting me, too. "No one could have stopped Cody from going on that expedition."

"I should have tried." Grandpa's white eyebrows cinched painfully. "But you were right. I was too ambitious. I wanted him to do all the mountains I couldn't. Everest. K2. Aconcagua. I pushed him. It was wrong of me. Terrible—" He couldn't go on, and looked at his feet.

Clumsily, I patted his back. "It wasn't your fault."

"You said so yourself."

"Grandpa . . ."

"You were right."

"No." For the first time in a long time, I saw things clearly. It was as if I'd been carrying a wrecking ball of rage and blame, looking for something to aim it at. Now I could see all the damage it had done—to me when I was carrying it, and to Grandpa when I let it loose.

The climbing harness dropped between us. He grabbed it and started fiddling with the straps. He knelt, holding it for me to step into, but I didn't. He shook the harness and said, "Come on. Let's go."

"Hold your horses, old man."

He dropped his hands and knelt there. He still wouldn't look at me, which actually made it easier for me to speak. "Sometimes I say things I don't mean, you know." He was stiff as he listened, perfectly still. "I'm just pissed off about the whole thing. About Cody."

"You don't have to explain." His voice was hoarse, defeated.

"Yes I do."

"No you don't." He stood, shook his head, but he still held his face away from me. "Water under the bridge."

"Shut up, you know?" I threw up my hands. "Half the time you won't talk and now you won't let me finish!"

"*I* don't talk? You've barely said two civil words to me since you got here!" Now he looked me in the eye, and he was mad.

My temper flared. "Well, I've been a little depressed."

"Join the club."

"You didn't seem too depressed at Darla's cabin the other day."

He glared at me.

"I shouldn't have said that."

He nodded once.

"You know, Grandpa, I'm just trying to tell you I'm sorry. Okay? I really am. For what I said yesterday." I paused, but he didn't respond. "I was wrong, and I didn't mean it."

He nodded again.

"Grandpa," I said harshly. He looked up at me. "Cody was a born climber, you said it yourself. If you hadn't taught him, he would have found another way. No one could have stopped him from going to Argentina."

The rope above us shook and a woman called down, "You in?"

I yelled impatiently, "Two minutes!" I looked at Grandpa, waiting for him to say something, but he just kept staring at the river below. "Grandpa? Did you hear me? It wasn't your fault. It wasn't anyone's fault. It just happened." I heard the truth in these words and realized I wasn't angry anymore, just deeply sad. "I'm sorry," I whispered.

"Okay." He mussed my hair, then knelt again to hold the harness for me. I stepped into it and he stood, tightening the strap around my waist, roughly tugging me. To keep my balance I had to put my hands on his shoulders. "You used to do this all the time for Cody, remember?"

We looked at each other for a moment, then Grandpa had to turn away again. "I miss that kid like hell," he said.

My voice crumbled into ashes. "Me too." Grandpa patted my head roughly, and we turned to look through the mist, each of us dropping our tears to the wind, an offering to the clamorous waters below.

30

Zachary's mother pulled him to her with a kind of animal desperation. Mabel cupped her plump hands over her tiny mouth, then burst into a huge smile when Zachary ran from his mother to her and gave her a big hug. Penny looked on, seeming to wilt a little until Zachary ran back to her and threw his little arms around her waist. Marcus looked on from Mabel's porch, his face slack. Then angry again. The warden turned on a deafening siren to call in all the search parties, and without a word got in his green pickup and drove off. Little by little, teams of tired searchers streamed in, red-eyed and battered. Nora rushed around passing out sack lunches and cookies from her restaurant, her cropped red hair bobbing through the crowd.

All eyes were on Zachary, who hid his face in his mother's blouse. The paramedics had already gone over him thoroughly, but Darla checked his fingers and the cuts on his face. She patted Penny's shoulder to re-assure her. Then she came at me with antiseptic and cotton balls. "Zachary's fine," she said. "But you're a mess." I sat on the porch while she worked me over, studying my expression as she dabbed at my scratches, then looking at Grandpa, who was devouring his second sack lunch from Nora, then back at me. After she wrapped my ankle in an Ace bandage, she got up and patted my shoulder. "Well done."

"It was dumb luck," I said, figuring if I told her a bear had led me to Zachary, she'd think I was nuts. I wasn't sure *I* didn't think I was nuts.

"I don't just mean Zachary, dear." She looked meaningfully over at Grandpa, who was laughing at something Ned had just said. "I don't know what you said, but you must have said something."

The air was still with the sureness of rain. The story of our rescue circulated through the crowd and I found myself being patted and jostled, congratulated and sized up, and the attention made me want to run inside and hide under Mabel's four-poster bed. A photographer from the local paper lined Zachary up with his family and took pictures, then took an endless stream of pictures of me with Zachary, me shaking a ranger's hand, me arm in arm with Grandpa, me alone standing under a tree. Finally, I snuck away and went to sit down, on Mabel's orange-flowered sofa, where I could rest my sore ankle and close my eyes.

I hadn't been alone for five minutes before I felt a hand on my shoulder. I looked up to see Penny standing over me. It was the first time I'd ever seen her close up. She was wiry like Marcus, small like Zachary, and so tired and aged that she could have been Mabel's sister. She pulled a long line of smoke out of her cigarette, and pushed it back out with a forceful sigh, sitting down on the chair across from me. "I'm Penny." Her voice was husky. She offered me her hand, and we shook. "It's nice to finally meet you," she said, then added, "Properly."

"Same here."

"I want to thank you for saving my baby."

"Of course."

She barely heard me. "I don't know what you must think. I don't know what Marcus has told you . . ." Her voice trailed off, her gaze unfocused, staring into empty space. "I just want you to know how much I love my sons."

"I can see that." I tried to smile at her, but she couldn't seem to look at me.

"If you hadn't let me talk to Zach, I really don't know how I would have gotten through the past weeks."

"He needed to talk to you, too."

She smiled at that, then her expression dimmed. "Nora said she'd give me a job in her restaurant."

"You're thinking of moving up here?"

She scoffed. "You think this valley is big enough for Mabel and me?"

"Well—" I felt uncomfortable, not sure what this woman wanted from me. "Nora's a good lady to work for."

"And Zachary loves Mabel," she said haltingly, a grim smile on her lips.

"He's a great kid," I said, because it seemed the only safe thing to say.

"Marcus seems to think highly of you." She took another pull on her cigarette and blew the smoke out through pursed lips, her eyes running up and down, reading me. "Can I ask you something?"

"Sure."

She put her fingers on her temple and rubbed at it nervously. "Do you think Marcus will ever be able to forgive me?"

What a question. I had never heard Marcus say anything about her that wasn't tinged with anger. I stuttered, "I—I know Marcus is angry with you, but I believe he loves you." Thinking of Grandpa, I added, "You can't get really mad at someone unless they mean something to you."

She nodded, taking another drag of smoke. Staring at the floor distantly, she muttered, "Marcus has a lot to be angry about."

We heard dozens of truck motors roaring to life outside, and rushed out to thank the volunteers. Slowly Mabel's driveway emptied. Soon, only Darla, Grandpa, Penny, Mabel, the boys and I sat in the living room, sunken boneless into over-soft furniture. Ned and Nora were still in the kitchen, packing up the coffee machine, washing dishes. The crickets murmured a cozy rhythm and we all let our eyelids droop. Grandpa and Darla were curled up together like two cats, and Grandpa was snoring softly.

The sun went down.

The front door creaked open slowly, and in walked Joseph. His gray hair was tangled with twigs and leaves. His eyes had shrunk into his skull from too much searching. He sent me a soft grin, then walked noiselessly over to Zachary and cupped a leathery hand over his cheek. He winked at Penny, who had stiffened at his approach, and held out his hand for her to shake. "I'm glad your little boy is safe," he said. She smiled.

Ned and Nora came into the living room, carrying a big box between them. When Ned saw Joseph he nearly dropped his end of the box. Nora swore softly. "Be careful!"

Joseph looked squarely at Ned, who seemed to shrink. Nora nodded at me and whispered, "You eat free the rest of the summer, kiddo."

I laughed. "You'll regret that."

She backed out the door, followed by Ned, who kept his head down.

Joseph watched out the window as the two of them loaded up Ned's truck and drove off. Then he slumped to the floor with exhaustion.

I looked over at Marcus, who was watching me with an odd expression. He cocked his head toward the door, and I followed him out onto the porch.

The air was sharp with the scent of snow up high.

He led me beyond the halo of light surrounding the cabin. "Annie," he muttered. Something in his voice sounded controlled, measured.

I kept my distance. "Yes?"

"I suppose you think I should apologize to you. For that phone call. And everything else. Right?"

I let my eyes wander over the dark lacy pattern of leaves against night clouds as I considered. He had been quiet all afternoon, even contrite, but there was something in his manner that still seemed angry. "You hurt my feelings."

"I know." He came toward me. I could hear his breath. In the darkness, his fingertips skirted over my face, found my lips.

He kissed me—long, salty, rough. My hands wandered up his straight back; his hands wound through my hair, pulling at it. Maybe it was going to be okay between us. I leaned into him, willingly losing myself, pulling him closer to me as he seemed to pull away.

And he pushed me off him. "When were you going to tell me?" His voice was as hard as his kiss had been.

I was still reeling, but his question set me further off balance. "What?"

"Mom mentioned her little phone calls to Zachary. At your place." Suddenly he was furious.

I was utterly confused. "I just—"

"You kept it from me. You *lied* to me."

"I thought—"

"What? That you had a right to meddle in my life?"

"Zachary wanted—" I couldn't understand this. He was kissing me one second and yelling at me the next. What was happening? "He needed her" was finally all I could say.

"And that was for you to decide?"

I stared at him, bewildered. "It was for *Zachary* to decide, Marcus."

He ignored this. "Now that everyone knows, there's no way we'll get out of here." Slouching, he was framed in a square of light that shone on him through the window of Mabel's house. His eyes were bitter on me.

I took a backward step toward the porch. "But your mom might be moving here. Things might turn out okay."

"So?"

"So there might not be a custody battle. You have no reason to go."

"Maybe you don't think so." He stood stiffly, hands in pockets, staring at me. I could see he was back to the dark Marcus, the dangerous Marcus. The side of him I'd learned to distrust. He moved out of the light and said, "I only hope Mom and Mabel don't press charges."

I remembered my conversation with Penny. "Marcus, I'm sure they've already forgiven you."

"You don't know my family, Annie. One second you think you can trust them, and then all of a sudden everything changes."

"Maybe if you *try* to trust them."

"I guess now that you're the big hero, you know what's best for everyone. Including my little brother."

"I'm just trying to talk to you." I hated how my voice sounded, quivering and weak.

He laughed bitterly and turned away from me, muttering, "Enjoy the limelight." And he was gone.

I stood listening to his steps down the path toward the river. Sucking in air to hold back tears, I sat down on the porch. I heard the front door open, someone approaching behind me, and Darla sat down next to me. "Anna, you were splendid today."

"I'm glad someone thinks so."

She smiled knowingly and put an arm around my shoulder. "I heard what Marcus said to you, and I'm not surprised by it."

"I am." I couldn't keep the hurt out of my voice. I'd always known it was a matter of time before he found out about Zachary talking to his Mom, but that didn't stop me from being really upset about his crazy, spiteful behavior. "Why does he want to hurt me?"

"Oh, God, Annie. I don't know. Maybe . . ." She wrapped her arm around me as she let loose a big sigh. "Maybe because for a long time Marcus was in charge of his family. When the boys came out here, he lost control. He had to compensate in some way for that, and look where that got him!"

"Why take it out on me?"

"Why does anyone do what they do? Maybe he wanted to be the one to find Zachary, to make right what he had done wrong. You took away his chance to do that."

"It's not fair."

"Give him time. He has a lot to work out right now."

"I know, but I thought I could help him."

She groaned at the sky. "How many women have uttered those words? It took me decades to learn that the only person in the world I can really be responsible for is myself. And believe me, I'm a handful."

She was trying to make me laugh, but I still felt like crying. "I feel so alone."

She surprised me by grabbing hold of my cheeks and kissing my forehead roughly. "Then stop isolating yourself and enjoy your life! You've only got one." She rose and pulled me up with her as she added, "As far as we know."

31

A huge root was poking into my spine, but I couldn't move. I'd been lying under the same tree in this miserable position for about ten minutes, stuck in a stalemate with a moose mother and her calf.

That's the problem with working in blinds. They're great to keep you hidden so you can get candid photos of animals, but if the animal discovers you hiding there and decides to take a stand, you're stuck in a tight spot. I'd chosen a young pine with low-hanging branches, stationed right next to a game trail. I heard mama's big hooves clomping before I saw her. I must have been pretty rusty still because I didn't check how close she was when I popped my lens cap off. The sound startled her so badly that she nearly ran over her baby backing away. Still nervous about turning her back to me, she kept one eye on me and one eye on her baby. She wasn't so concerned that she couldn't chew on some greens while she waited to see what I was up to. I could take my chances and stand up, but she was only about five feet away, and if I startled her, she might decide to kick me in the head.

Moose can be persnickety.

I had no choice but to stay right where I was, lying with my Nikon on my chest and a pine root grinding into my back. I'd gotten more close-up moose portraits than I could afford to get developed. Still, every so often, Mama stopped chewing to give me a suspicious sideways glance, and it looked so cute I couldn't resist snapping another frame. What else was I going to do?

Mom had brought my camera with her when she came up for the weekend a few weeks ago. I'd been nervous about seeing her because the past six months had been so painful for both of us. I was reading a book when I heard the tires of her Jeep pull into the driveway. She looked sad when she got out of the car, probably because it was her first time back at the cabin since Cody died. I saw she'd gotten a haircut. Her wavy gray hair was shoulder length again, and it suited her. She seemed to have put some of her weight back on, and though her once vivid eyes were still subdued by loss, the dark circles had faded a bit. She looked like Mom again. I watched through the front window as Grandpa rushed out to help her with her bag. He kissed her hello, and the two of them hugged close for a long time. When she saw me come through the front door, her teary eyes brightened up at once. We both laughed and cried as we hugged, and she whispered, "I missed you so, Annie."

"Me too," I said.

"I brought you a present." She bent into the car and pulled out my Nikon in its case, along with a beautiful new wide angle lens, still in the box.

I'd figured she would bring it with her, but I didn't know how happy I would be to see my camera again.

It was a nice visit, and too short. Both Grandpa and I were sorry she could only stay a couple nights, but I was glad she came. For the first time since losing Cody, I felt I had a home again.

Suddenly Mama Moose jerked to attention and

turned her ears backward to listen. Baby moved a little closer to her, leaning against her firm brown side. I lay still.

Footsteps were coming down the trail.

I kept my eyes on Mama, who seemed unsure what to do. I was afraid she might suddenly reassess me as a threat and decide to stomp on my face. After a tense moment, though, she simply trotted off with her baby, disappearing into the shelter of the trees.

I listened again for the footsteps, but they'd stopped altogether. Perhaps the hiker turned onto a different trail.

I started to pull myself up off the ground.

A shadow moved over me.

I yelped.

Joseph knelt down to peer at me under the tree branches. "Boo."

"Joseph! You scared me!" I exclaimed. He chuckled and offered me a hand to help me up. My left leg was asleep, and I could still feel that damn pine root in my back, but it was heaven to be able to move again. "Where have you been?" I asked. I hadn't seen him since that last night at Mabel's cabin.

"Around," he said, and pointed at my camera. "Want to take my picture?"

"Not really," I said as I trained my lens on him, working the focus to emphasize the wrinkles around his eyes.

"Do it like this." He folded his arms over his chest and offered his profile, a perfect portrait of an American Indian man staring serenely at the horizon.

"Come off it, Joseph," I said. He winked at me and started laughing, and that's when I snapped his picture. "What are you doing here?" I asked him.

"I was looking for you."

I raised my eyebrows at him skeptically. "So you started wandering randomly through the forest?"

"I went to your grandfather's to talk to you. He said you would be looking for animals and showed me your footprints out the door. Easy." He held up his beautiful buckskin pipe bag and said, "Want to go to our tree?"

"That's my brother's tree," I corrected him, even though I'd started thinking of it as Zachary's tree. Almost every day since we found him, he'd asked me to take him there. I think he wanted to be absolutely sure of where it was so he would never get lost again. I didn't mind. It was a good place to hang out and read, and I found the more I went there, the easier it was to remember Cody without becoming overwhelmed with sadness.

We followed the trail at a slow gait. It didn't take long before the game trail merged into a larger path, which took us, weaving, to the meadow where the Tepee Tree stood. It seemed as if all trails led to this place.

Joseph held up the branches for me, and I stepped in. I winced when I saw a candy bar wrapper lying on the ground, and snatched it up before Joseph could see it. I would have to mention this to Zachary. He had to be more careful.

Joseph sat down across from me, his elbows wrapped around his knees, fingers woven together. I sat cross-legged and leaned my chin in my hands. I figured he had something to tell me, but I knew he'd take his time getting to it.

"That little boy will remember you the rest of his life," he finally said with a grin.

I figured he must mean Zachary. "We've spent a lot of time together."

"He will remember you as the person who saved his life."

"Yeah," I mumbled. I'd been congratulated enough for what had happened. It was nice being called a hero, but I was ready to put it behind me. I'd never liked being the center of attention. "I was just lucky."

"Lucky you followed that bear?" He sniggered when he saw the surprised look on my face.

I had kept that bear a secret all summer long. I just couldn't talk about it, first because I'd been unsure of how to describe what happened, but then because I was unsure that it had happened at all. I'd been pushed so far past my limits, looking back on that day was like trying to remember a dream. Part of me didn't want to believe that I had really stood on that ledge, face to face with the bear, breathing her scent as she breathed mine. It was crazy behavior. "How did you know about that?"

"When I was out searching, I found your tracks near grizzly tracks, then I saw the boy's tracks on the trail along with many others. That's how I knew he'd been found."

I said nothing. Having someone know about it made me feel exposed. Once again, Joseph had pushed me off balance.

"Did she have a message for you?" Joseph asked tentatively.

I could see he was dying to know what happened, so I said nothing—just stared back into his tawny eyes.

He laughed softly.

I wished I could laugh too, but I felt too shaky, too confused. Had there been a vision? Had I gotten a message? "Joseph, I don't really know what happened. I don't understand it."

"Join the club." His eyes cinched into painful slits. "These things take a lifetime to understand, I think."

I studied him for a moment, wondering about the sadness that seemed to color everything he said. "Why did you go looking for a message?"

He raised his eyebrows at me and shrugged. "I don't really know."

It was my turn to be enigmatic and piercing. "Something happened. Something made you come to this valley," I said.

He watched me carefully, sizing me up, then shrugged again. "My wife left me."

"Where did she go?"

"She moved in with her sister."

"Why?"

He passed his palm over his cheek. "I don't know."

"She didn't tell you?"

He shook his head. "Maybe I didn't pay enough attention to her."

That's what I had always thought about Grandpa, that he hadn't paid attention to me. He and I had ignored each other for so long. But things had slowly gotten easier as the summer progressed. I no longer felt so uncomfortable being quiet with him, and even started to appreciate the space. Grandpa knows how to let a person be—sometimes too much. "Did you ask her *why* she left you, Joseph?"

He squinted at me. "You're just a kid." Obviously he could dish out a probing question, but he couldn't take one.

"Did you?" I asked again. Suddenly I wasn't intimidated by him anymore. Now that I knew something about his life, he didn't seem like the shaman who knew better than everyone else. Joseph was just a regular guy with regular problems. "Joseph, tell me you asked her."

He looked at me, blank.

"So you came here to ask a bear?"

He shrugged. "It's my way." His eyes glided off me to rest on the pine needles we sat on.

I nodded as I slowly screwed my lens cap onto my camera. "You know, Joseph . . ."—I paused, waiting until his eyes were on my face again. With a smirk I couldn't control, I said, "A she-bear can kill you just as dead as a boar."

He chuckled grimly as he pulled out his pipe tobacco. "I know it."

32

When I got home it was nightfall. Grandpa still wasn't home.

I took a long shower to get the smoke smell out of my hair, then went up to the loft for my pajamas. I opened the top drawer of my dresser to find the bear pendant Grandpa had given me after that first day on the river. It seemed so long ago, but it had only been a couple of months since I'd first encountered Great-Grandmother. I held the red jasper between my palms, warming the stone, then slipped the leather thong over my head. I liked the weight of the pendant—my totem—on my breastbone.

I thought about Joseph and his wife, how he never even asked her why she left. It reminded me of Grandma's letters, how far away she'd gotten from Grandpa, and how he hadn't noticed. He'd probably just let her be, hoping the problems would sort themselves out. It's too easy for people to lose each other.

I heard the yelp of Grandpa's truck engine as he threw it into park.

I decided I'd let him be for long enough.

I rooted in the hallway closet until I found what I was looking for. I was setting it up on the kitchen table when he came in, rubbing his hip. He saw me sitting there, and a big smile broke over his face.

"I call red."

He sat down across from me and set up his marbles. "One game."

"You always say that."

He grinned again and made the first move.

I had overtaken five of his men when I could finally come out with it. "You know, I found some letters in the cabinet a while ago." I checked his face for signs that the topic was off-limits, but he was staring at the board.

Finally his eyes shot up at me for a split second. "Oh?"

"Yeah." I waited for another minute, too afraid to say it. But it was now or never. "Between you and Grandma."

He paused and I thought he would blow his lid, but he just said, "Oh. Those letters." He leaned back in his chair and looked at the board again as if we were done talking about it.

I took his forward soldier and waited a few moves. By the time I figured out how to ask, he had shifted the balance of power and I was pretty much cornered. I only had another few moves before my forces would be crushed and I would have to admit defeat. Tentatively, I started, "You know, Joseph told me his wife left him."

"Oh good. He found you then," he said, but kept his eyes trained on the board.

"I was trying to think of a way to tell him how he could get her back."

He took another of my men before muttering, "Tell him to beg."

"What?"

"Tell him to get in his damn truck and drive to wherever she is and beg her to come back."

"Is that what you did? You drove to Chicago?"

Again he was silent, and I thought he would yell at me for intruding. But all he said was, "Yup."

"In your truck?"

"Yup."

"In February?"

"Before the interstate highway system."

"You drove to Chicago and begged her to come back."

"Yup."

"And then what?"

He took my last piece before saying, "You're awfully nosy."

Typical Jack McGraw response. "You know," I said, "you don't exactly come off smelling like a rose in those letters."

Suddenly he pushed the board away and got up from the table. "You invaded my privacy."

"I didn't realize what I was reading at first. I'm sorry."

This seemed to appease him. He leaned on the counter by the sink, staring into space.

"Now that I know," I continued hesitantly, "you can explain. What happened?" I waited at the table, trembling a little at the thought of how far I'd gone. This conversation stretched back through decades, a long hard road over dusty trails and ashes. But I was going to finish it, even if it meant an intrusion, even if it meant opening a wound. I needed to know what happened to my grandmother, her life with this man who represented fathoms I'd always been afraid of. "Grandpa, please."

He stood in the dark corner of the kitchen, looking at me. He was breathing a little hard as he leaned against the pine counter that had been carved by his father as a wedding gift for his wife. He cleared his throat. "She got Mabel to drive her to the train station in Pocatello. She left that note on the bed." His voice seemed to dry up and he paused, took a deep breath. "I waited. Truth is, I didn't believe it at first. I thought she'd get to the train station and turn right around. It just didn't seem like her. But she didn't come back. And then I got mad, and for a while I tried to pretend it didn't matter to me. But it did. You can't pretend things like that for too long. Not if you want to stay . . . living."

I'd never heard him talk like this before. It was so painful, the way his voice was small, the way he seemed to wilt, I almost wished I hadn't done this to him. But I couldn't stop him. I turned away, knowing he would talk easier if I wasn't looking.

"I guess I'm stubborn. I always have been. It takes a kind of stubbornness to live here, or it did, back then. But that's no excuse. My wife couldn't live with me and that burned a hole through me. So finally I borrowed some money off my dad, and I gassed up the pickup, and Mom gave me enough cold chicken to get me a good part of the way there, and I drove. It took me four days, but that was pretty good time back then. Especially on those roads." He shook his head. "Her dad didn't want to let me in. So first I had to beg *him*. I told him I loved his daughter and I deserved a chance, and I waited in the cold until my hands were numb, but finally the door opened. It was her mom who let me in. And I went upstairs to your grandmother and I found her sitting in a rocking chair with your mother in her lap, and she was crying, dark circles under her eyes. She looked bad. She looked . . . sad." He paused as if waiting for an ache to pass. "I think I split down the middle looking at her like that. And I know I started—Well, I cried a little too." He said this gruffly, angrily, and I wondered if he was crying as he told me the story, but I didn't dare turn around to look. "So I went up to her and I got on my knees and I told her I loved her and I couldn't live without her and my daughter, and I begged her, Annie. What can I say? I begged. And we drove back home and . . ." He trailed off, faded, but finally said, "I tried harder."

I sat looking at the leftovers of our game, imagining the long road of my grandparents' marriage. It was a distance I couldn't grasp. Not yet.

We were both quiet until Grandpa stirred. Slowly, he pulled out the chair across from me and sat down. "Annie?" I raised my eyes to his face. I'd never seen him so sad. "What you said. About how I—" He swallowed. "How I favored Cody."

I waited, not really wanting to hear, but unable to say anything to stop him.

"I've been thinking about it. I've thought it over every day since." He leaned his elbows on the table, nodding a little. "I treated you different. I see that now."

"Yeah, well." I tried to wave it away, but Grandpa wasn't going to let me out of it.

"It's just, he was easier to talk to. I didn't know what to say to a little girl. It's no excuse—"

"Do we have to—"

"You never seemed to need me anyway. You were always inside your books and pictures. You were quiet like me. And I'm not one to initiate conversation."

"Yeah, well—"

"But I always loved you." He was looking at me, his eyes pleading. "Every bit as much as I loved Cody. Still do."

I could only nod.

Far away, an owl murmured in the night.

I thought about how angry I'd been at Grandpa, for most of my life. I had good reason to be angry. He did favor Cody, and he had finally admitted it. I remembered Marcus, the way he'd snarled at me outside Mabel's cabin, how he was stubbornly clinging to his rage even though his family was trying to get better. I hadn't heard a word from him since the day we found Zachary. At first I felt hopeful he would come by Grandpa's so we could talk, but after a few weeks with no sign of him, I didn't really want to see him anymore. He seemed so selfish to me, so bitter and mean.

I didn't want to be that way.

The cabin seemed to settle a little closer in. After a while of sitting there, letting Grandpa's words float down to rest like dust on the surfaces of the room, I could finally look at him. I raised my eyebrows and said, "Two out of three?"

Epilogue

Like old times, we played Chinese checkers way past bedtime. It was late when I climbed up the ladder to the loft.

The night was clear and cool, and I could see a million stars out the window. I imagined my brother as one of them. I hung my grizzly bear pendant on the wall next to my favorite picture of Cody. It was one of the only pictures that really showed how brilliant his smile was, and it made me think about the old African belief that a photograph captures a piece of your soul.

I lay on my cot. The crickets were singing up a storm, and the moon was starting to roll over the horizon, full and bright. I closed my eyes. Soon I would be back in Denver, with no starry sky to fill my window, no cricket song.

All I will have in my room will be the dark.

The dark and the noise of civilization.

And my memories.

And my dreams.

✝ ✝ ✝

She stands like a monument to strength, staring at me over her great shoulder, lips parted in a snarl or a grin. This grizzly is equal to anything. I get up from the forest floor, barefoot, my eyes sore from tears or laughter, my hands rough from labor or play.

I ask no questions.

Birds swirl like a fluttering symphony, through and into and above the branches of the trees. The grizzly moves through the living curtain of feathered wings, wandering with sure steps through the forest. I follow behind her, afraid of what I will find in the meadow. He will be standing with his back to me, his hands in his pockets. The skin on him will be mottled and patchy. He will be shriveled, decayed.

I will see him there. The awful truth of him, of what he has become.

Cody is dead.

Silently, Great-Grandmother parts the trees.

I shake my head, but her snout shoves me forward. Still, I cannot look. My eyes on the ground, I walk into the meadow toward where I know he will be. My steps are slow, my heart aching with each pulse of my blood.

Finally I reach it, the center of this meadow where the cruel shadow falls, and I stop, my eyes cast down. He is here with me. He will always be with me. He must be here, but I still cannot raise my eyes to him.

I look back at Great-Grandmother. She is dancing behind me, bobbing her great head, stamping her paws on the soft ground. Birds whirl above her, butterflies twirl at her feet. Trees sway together in a rhythm cadenced to the spinning earth.

Finally I have the courage. I can raise my head to look at Cody, my dead brother.

But he isn't here. This meadow is empty.

He's gone. Cody is gone.

A long wail sounds, hollow and forlorn. It issues from my throat, jagged and broken and infinitely sad.

I stand in this empty meadow, weeping for my brother, for what I've lost, for everything he lost.

A cool breeze whispers in the blackened branches of the trees, stirring this clearing in shadow.

I lift my face to the sun.

And the shadow falls away.